There'

Razmar glanced up at the baby's wicker basket lying behind Malik and further up the slope of the roof. "How's the princess doing, Malik?"

"She's quite well, actually. She's taking her morning nap. Thank you for inquiring about her health." Malik was silent for a moment. "You know, it's so peaceful, I might just have to kill anybody who interrupts her nap." *Because she'll want to be fed*, he thought, *and she'll cry, and I don't have anything for her.*

"You're a good man, Malik. It would be a shame if we had to kill you."

"You can try. You may recall that I left a bunch of your men on the stairway as we retreated up here."

"I know. I was impressed." Razmar chuckled ruefully. "Impressed, but still appalled. Still, here you are now. Injured. Making your heroic last stand on the roof of this tower. How long do you think you can last?"

"Long enough."

"You know you can only delay the inevitable. The princess is going to die no matter what. The only real question is whether you die, too."

"At least I won't be a traitor," Malik replied.

Books by David Keener

Pivot Point *
Road Trip
An Unlikely Hero
The Whispering Voice

The Thousand Kingdom Series

Bitter Days
Death Comes to Town *
The Rooftop Game
Stone Spirits *

Inflection Point Universe

Banner Yet Waves *
Clash by Night
Dustbowl Detective *
Finders Keepers *

As Editor

Fantastic Defenders
Fantastic Detectives
The Forever Inn *

Forthcoming

The Rooftop Game

David Keener

Tannhauser Press

The Rooftop Game

"The Rooftop Game" originally published in *Worlds Enough: Fantastic Defenders*, May 2017
"Winter Roses" originally published in *Uncommon Threads*, June 2015

Tannhauser Press
www.tannhauserpress.com
Fredericksburg, VA 22407

ISBN: 978-1-945994-17-3

Packaging by Worlds Enough LLC
Cover Design by Don Anderson
Copyediting by Donna Royston

For my Dad, who would have loved
the movie of this story

Widow's Tower, Fortress Paksenaral.
In Lantille, Salasia, near the Cragenrath
Mountains.

CONTENTS

PART I

OPENING MOVES

I. NOW

*In the opening, achieving positional advantage is
paramount.*

— Karkomir, Grand Master, from Salasia

Lydio Malik lay on his back on the sloped roof of
the Widow's Tower, the tallest tower of Paksenaral, the
ancestral fortress of the Burgundar line. He tried to
relax, to take advantage of this brief respite in the
fighting and rest his tired, aching muscles. He crossed
his hands behind his neck and looked up at the sky. A
few puffy white clouds glided gently across the vault of
blue, guided inexorably by the autumn winds toward
the Cragenrath Mountains, violet and robbed of detail
in the distance. The sky seemed so peaceful, so at odds
with everything going on below.

Lowering his gaze, Malik saw smoke billowing up
from the numerous fires consuming Lantille, the wind

bending the smoke towards the mountains like a dark and ragged banner. The city's Gladis Market was a raging inferno; the blocks of wooden merchant stands, livestock holding facilities, and tenements were all burning. There were fires down by the river, as well. The docks, a few ships, and a number of nearby warehouses were ablaze. Other ships had cast free and were fleeing the fires and the fighting.

The most worrisome fires to Malik, though, were the ones on the far periphery of the small city that marked the headquarters, support buildings, and barracks of Lantille's militia. He didn't think there'd be any help coming from that direction, at least not anytime soon.

In Malik's estimation, the attack had been a meticulously planned "smash-and-kill" raid utilizing a limited number of Kashmal rebels, probably no more than a few hundred men, and carefully timed to take advantage of King Salzari's excursion to the north. The enemy's undetected infiltration into Lantille, and into the fortress, strongly implied insider help. Given the widespread mayhem, he concluded that the effort had almost certainly been supported by at least one combat mage.

If the Kashmal had possessed mages, they'd have used them in the failed rebellion two years ago. So, the mage represented foreign aid to the rebels. Malik could almost sense unseen forces moving pieces on a chessboard and aligning them against King Salzari, and against Salasia.

He found his fingers toying with the makeshift rope that was his lifeline. The rope was made of strips cut from sheets and tied together. One end of the rope was tied around his waist and the other looped around the spire of the tower. He had a certain amount of play in the rope, so he could move around the circular roof with its rippled, orange tiles and even stand without worrying about tumbling nine stories to his death.

Come to think of it, falling was probably the least of his worries.

He could hear the sounds of fighting somewhere in the fortress below, the clashing of swords, a few shouts and screams, and an explosion every once in a while. The rebels hadn't taken the fortress yet, but it wouldn't be long.

When the sounds of fighting were done, he suspected the Queen would be dead. They'd be coming for him next.

Malik sat up and drew his sword out of its sheath. A thin strip of cloth was tied to the pommel; the other end was tied to his right wrist. He couldn't afford to drop the sword and have it slide off the roof. There was undoubtedly more edgework in the offing.

Unless an enemy mage turned up and roasted him. Still, you could only plan for the things you could control. If a mage showed up, then the game was over, and that was it.

He eyed his blade critically. It was clearly showing some severe wear. There were numerous nicks in the blade and, although he'd wiped it off, there were still traces of blood around some of the nicks. Well, he didn't think he was going to live long enough to worry about the blade rusting.

He tested the edge with his thumb. Dull.

It had been sharp earlier this morning.

Malik reached into a pocket, took out a file and began sharpening the blade.

Time was the only thing on Malik's side. The enemy hadn't brought enough forces to hold the fortress for any significant time, especially if they wanted to escape the storm that would be coming their way. Even now, any remaining militiamen were probably rallying. Calls were likely going out to nearby towns for armed help. The garrison at Evanscap wasn't that far away either. If he had to guess, the King would hear about this mess by evening. And he had mages.

A soft gurgle came from above him. He raised his head and watched as Princess Analisa, all of seven months old and heir to the throne of Salasia, shifted sleepily in her basket. The royal basket, as he liked to think of it, was suspended above him on the roof, where the slope increased dramatically. Like him, the basket was attached to the spire by a makeshift rope. Additional cloth strips were tied around the princess' basket to ensure that she didn't fall out.

It was too bad that escape hadn't been an option. He'd have to hold out as long as he could.

Lydio Malik, Royal Bodyguard for Princess Analisa, resumed sharpening his sword and waited for the enemy's next move.

II. FOUR MONTHS AGO

I feel as if I were a piece in a game of chess, when my opponent says of it: That piece cannot be moved.

— Soren the Mad, Grand Master, from Zembelis

Salzari Rukitar, the King of Salasia, walked the labyrinthine halls of his family's ancestral fortress, flanked by his bodyguards and trailed, as always, by his secretary and a gaggle of advisors. Still vigorous at forty-seven, he walked quickly, the less fit among his retinue scurrying to keep up.

He was a little irked at the interruption in his routine that his next appointment had caused. Tradition required his presence, but he was a busy man and had many calls upon his time. There was a reason he delegated whenever he could. Despite the ubiquitous government bureaucracy, the kingdom didn't exactly run itself. Somebody had to make the difficult decisions, like what to do about the unsettled situation in the north.

Two years since their failed rebellion, and the Kashmal tribes were still making trouble. Oh, they'd been soundly defeated in battle, and he'd been suitably harsh with the terms and penalties in the aftermath, but he'd stopped well short of the butchery that other rulers might have engaged in.

He wrenched his thoughts away from the Kashmal situation to focus on his next appointment. As he walked, he said, "Winton, you've read the particulars. What do you think of them?"

His secretary, struggling to keep up, puffed beside him. "Sire, they're excellent as always. Interestingly, there are six candidates this time instead of the usual five. There was a tie for fifth in the competition."

"A tie, you say? That hasn't happened in years. Since I was a child, in fact."

Old Napotan, his father's favorite guardsman, had retired, opening up a slot in the elite Phoenix Guard. Capped at only two hundred members, the competition for the open position had been fierce. For the first time, he'd understood that the royal guardsmen he'd always taken for granted were indeed the best of the best. Some of them served as personal bodyguards for the royal family. Others functioned as royal investigators, the eyes and ears of the King.

"The best fighter is the Yallon fellow," Winton said, his glasses sliding partway down his nose. "He's a beast, a real giant of a man, and the overall leader in points. But a little thick, I think. The Neferian is interesting. Lydio Malik…"

Kanlo Mudelsen, a trade advisor, interjected, "Certainly not the Neferian. He's lucky he even got this far." Kanlo shook his head, his long gray hair whipping from side to side, seemingly emphasizing his comment. "Quite frankly, he's not even in the same class as the others."

"That doesn't even make sense, Kanlo," the mousy-looking secretary responded. "He's here because he tied for fifth in points. All earned fairly, I might add."

"I agree with him, though," said Pavel Gundarsen, Salzari's political strategist. "The Neferian would send the wrong political message. We're already getting inundated by thousands of refugees from their vicious little war. They're coming across the straits in anything that floats. Appointing a Neferian would simply encourage more refugees to come here. Not to mention, they're losing. Badly. Do we want to send a message to the winners that we support the Neferians?"

Salzari said, "We do believe in the Neferian cause." There was silence for a moment.

Winton said, "Pavel, the Neferian is actually a fourth-generation Salasian. He's served in the army, where he distinguished himself in battle. Mustered out, joined the City Guard, and has a sterling reputation as a crime investigator."

A servant rushed ahead of the group to open a wide, ornately carved wooden door. Salzari and his retinue walked through the door into bright sunshine and made their way through the south gardens to the Phoenix Compound, which included their head-quarters building, barracks, and stables.

Captain Perin Davani, the gray-haired leader of the Phoenix Guard, greeted Salzari and his retinue as they arrived at the training area, a grass field adjacent to the barracks building and outlined by a three-bar wooden fence. About fifteen guardsmen sat on the fence, waiting to observe the selection. The six candidates stood at attention in the training area, ranked in order of points. Salzari noticed that they'd placed the Malik fellow, notable because of his darker skin, almost like a permanently dark tan, at the very end on the right. Yallon was obviously the huge man on the left, head and shoulders taller than the others, none of whom would have normally been described as small.

Salzari asked Captain Davani, "Who do you favor?"

"Sire, I'd recommend Kelson. Second in points, but sharp as a new nail. The leader, Yallon, well, he's a good fighter, but that's all he is."

Salzari turned to Denzi Trufar, his military advisor and the only one who hadn't yet weighed in on the choices. "And you, Denzi. You've been quiet so far. Your recommendation?"

"I like Malik, Sire. He's not the best of the fighters out there, but he learns the fastest."

Salzari approached the candidates to examine them more closely. Saying nothing, he strolled down the line. The men stayed at attention, staring straight forward.

The king strode back to Captain Davani. "I'd like to see Yallon and Malik fight," he said loudly for the benefit of the audience. "Unarmed."

Davani barked a few orders. The other candidates assumed positions on the fence, looking a little disconcerted at seeing their own chances vanishing. Salzari glanced at his timepiece to note the time as Yallon and Malik faced off in the grass.

Yallon made the first move, a powerful roundhouse punch that missed badly. Malik counter-punched him with a quick flurry of strikes to Yallon's torso that didn't seem to hurt him too much. After a few minutes, Salzari noticed that Malik was controlling the pace of the fight, moving around, trying to tire Yallon and, most importantly, staying out of Yallon's reach. The fight could easily be lost if Yallon was able to turn it into a wrestling match where his size and strength could be used to maximum advantage.

Five minutes into the bout, Yallon managed to land a vicious uppercut to Malik's jaw that stunned him momentarily. Yallon pressed his advantage and pounded his torso unmercifully while he held his arms up to protect his head. The powerful blows knocked Malik off his feet. Yallon stepped forward, preparing to jump on him. Malik kicked him in the knee that he'd just put all his weight on. Malik rolled to the side as

Yallon yelled in pain and fell full-length onto the ground.

Malik got to his feet, holding one arm across his damaged ribs, and landed a few hard kicks on Yallon before the giant, grimacing in obvious agony, climbed to his feet.

After ten minutes of continuous fighting, which Salzari verified by checking his timepiece, both fighters were a sweating, bloody mess. Malik was circling the less mobile giant, hunched over to protect his ribs, and striking whenever he saw an opening.

Malik lunged in with a flurry of jabs. Yallon absorbed the punches, then pounded through Malik's defenses before the smaller man could back away. Yallon delivered a powerful blow to Malik's ribs, eliciting an agonized scream of pain. The giant head-butted Malik in the face, breaking the smaller man's nose, grabbed his shoulders to hold him in place, and drove a knee into Malik's stomach. While Yallon was momentarily supported only by the leg with the knee he'd hurt earlier, Malik kicked it again and it promptly collapsed. Yallon fell on top of the Neferian.

Raising his upper body with his left hand, Yallon began pounding Malik in the head with his right fist. When he was satisfied with the result, he finally rolled off the smaller fighter. With his damaged knee, it took him a while to get back to his feet. He faced the King and his companions, raised his arms triumphantly, and seemed surprised when nobody cheered.

He looked behind him. Somehow, Malik was on his feet again. Wobbly, yes, but definitely standing. Hunched over in pain, his face almost obscured by blood, the smaller warrior made a "come hither" gesture with his hands when he saw Yallon looking at him.

Salzari said in a voice loud enough to be heard across the field, "Enough." Both men were already so badly battered that he'd have to engage the Royal Healer to heal them properly. And he'd seen everything he needed to see.

Turning to Captain Davani, Salzari said, "I've made my decision." He pointed at the candidate he'd chosen. "That one. No, not the big one. The other one. Malik. I like him. He doesn't give up."

III. NOW

Chess is ruthless; you've got to be prepared to kill people.

— Nunzio Cragenrath, Grand Master, from
  Cragenrath

Malik looked on curiously as a hand holding a silk handkerchief trimmed in lace rose above the roof's edge. The hand waved the handkerchief back and forth a few times, as if to ensure that it had caught his attention. The hand and the makeshift flag withdrew below the roofline, and a moment later, a man's head appeared in the same place.

Malik raised his eyebrows when he recognized Tulis Razmar, Lantille's Chief of Trade. His presence confirmed Malik's conjecture that the attackers had benefited from insider help. Thanks to Razmar's betrayal, he was reasonably sure that the man's direct liege lord and, supposedly, close personal friend, Callum Burgundar, was already dead, and most likely the Queen, too. So much for oaths.

"Good morning, Lydio," Razmar said with an easy, friendly smile, acting as if there was nothing unusual about meeting on a rooftop. "Do you mind if I climb up so we can talk?"

"You can sit on the edge. The first five rows of tile. Try anything...I'll gut you like a fish."

Razmar climbed very carefully onto the roof. He was a tall man in his forties but still fit, clean-shaven, with close-cropped hair liberally infused with gray. He wore fancy leggings and what looked like a bright-colored tunic, now mostly covered by the leather armor he'd added to his ensemble.

"Infernally good view up here, my friend," Razmar said.

"Yes, we can see most of your handiwork from up here," Malik replied, making a sweeping gesture with his left hand, his non-sword hand, to encompass the fires raging throughout the city. He stood, one leg higher than the other on the slanted roof, holding his makeshift rope with his left hand for balance and leaving his right hand free for swordplay if necessary. He could feel blood trickling slowly down the back of his leg.

Razmar shrugged. "Sometimes it's necessary to take actions we regret in order to pursue a greater good."

"That being what?"

"Karsh, the whole Kashmal region, Lantille, we're going to form our own kingdom."

"I doubt it." Malik looked at him levelly. "For what you've done today, King Salzari is going to crush you like a grape under a blacksmith's hammer."

Razmar laughed. "He can try. We've got serious backing."

Interesting. Malik was sure the King would love to know about these mysterious backers. Meanwhile, Malik was willing to talk for as long as Razmar wanted. The more time the traitor wasted, the better for him, and for Princess Analisa.

As if reading his mind, the older man glanced up at the baby's wicker basket lying behind Malik and further up the slope of the roof. "How's the princess doing, Malik?"

"She's quite well, actually. She's taking her morning nap. Thank you for inquiring about her health." Malik was silent for a moment. "You know, it's so peaceful, I might just have to kill anybody who interrupts her nap." *Because she'll want to be fed*, he thought, *and she'll cry, and I don't have anything for her.*

"You're a good man, Malik. It would be a shame if we had to kill you."

"You can try. You may recall that I left a bunch of your men on the stairway as we retreated up here."

"I know. I was appalled." Razmar chuckled ruefully. "Impressed, but still appalled. Still, here you are now. Injured. Wearing damaged leather armor. Making your heroic last stand on a hot tile roof. How long do you think you can last?"

"Long enough."

"You know you can only delay the inevitable. The princess is going to die no matter what. The only real question is whether you die, too."

"At least I won't be a traitor," Malik replied.

"Oh, that hurts. I prefer to think of myself as a patriot for a grand new kingdom." Razmar laughed easily.

"Just out of curiosity, why do you want to kill the princess?" Malik asked politely. "I would have thought you'd want her as a hostage. Better chance of negotiation with the King that way."

Razmar paused for a moment, as if thinking about whether he should answer the question. He shrugged. "It's a condition from our backers. They want the King's line ended."

"Ah. So what happens if your backers get what they want? How long do you think they'll keep supporting a bunch of lost-cause, would-be kingdom builders?"

Razmar laughed. "Let's just say that our mutual interests are well aligned. You should worry more about your situation than ours." To emphasize his point, the older man looked around the roof. "One last time, will you give us the princess?"

"No."

"Well, we're going to have to kill you then."

Malik shrugged. "Bring it on."

Razmar shook his head in mock regret. Malik watched impassively as the older man climbed slowly and gingerly down from the roof.

Two of his borrowed Kashmal fighters helped Razmar back through the window. He was sweating from the exertion of climbing. Growing up in the shadow of the Cragenrath Mountains, he'd done some rock climbing when he was a younger man, but facing that sheer, nine-story drop on the way back had been more daunting than any climb he'd ever done. Going up was easier than coming back down, though not by much.

He straightened his clothing self-consciously, then looked around. There were ten Kashmal warriors with him in a fancy bedroom, including his second-in-command, Pandomar, a stocky, red-haired warrior. One thing for sure, Pandomar wouldn't be doing any climbing; he'd lost most of his left arm at the Battle of Antigon two years before.

A pair of warriors were guarding Melly Scarp, the royal nanny, who managed to look both defiant and scared at the same time.

"You," he said, pointing at one of the warriors. "Get up there and kill him. He's injured. He's got so much blood pouring down his right leg, it's a wonder he can even stand."

The fighter looked at Pandomar, who nodded slightly. The man moved obediently towards the window.

"You're not going to beat Malik that easily," Melly interjected from across the room.

Razmar laughed. "Perhaps not." He turned to Pandomar. "Let's put some archers in the south tower."

"Ser, we didn't bring any archers."

Razmar sighed. "An oversight. I'm sure that the Burgundars have some bows here somewhere. Find them. Find someone who knows how to shoot them. Put them in the south tower." The Kashmal were useful, but sometimes they had no imagination.

Pandomar gestured to one of the younger warriors. "Nakanti, handle it."

"Yes, Father," the youth said. He turned and strode from the room.

The Kashmal fighter heaved himself over the roof's edge, lunged to a standing position, drew his sword, and stepped toward Malik.

The fighter's forward boot slipped on the wet tile where Malik had urinated only a few moments before. He fell forward, audibly cracking his chin as he landed face-first on the orange roof tiles. Stunned, he dropped his sword, which slid off the roof, followed almost immediately by the screaming rebel warrior.

A few seconds later, there was a thud and clatter as the fighter hit the ground below.

Malik couldn't help grinning. All of his fights should be that easy.

Danteel the silversmith had closed up his small shop hours ago. He'd carried in his display tables, pulled down the shutters, and latched them securely. He'd even taken down the shop sign. There was a battle going on in the city and, even though he didn't know what was going on or who was fighting, it was best to make sure his shop didn't look like it would be worth looting.

Danteel was a prudent man. A cautious man.

His shop was fairly typical, a three-story wooden building with a high, peaked roof. What was most important, though, was its location, which happened to be close to Paksenaral, the fortress that dominated the city of Lantille, and, by extension, its residents, most of whom could afford his prices. He and his family lived on the upstairs floors, with the downstairs serving as a common room at night and his shop during the day.

Danteel didn't like not knowing what was going on. Prudent men didn't like surprises.

What worried him right now, though, was his thirteen-year-old son. Chanama had bargained with Danteel for some time off that morning to visit the Gladis Market with some of his friends. He was still out there somewhere.

Whatever was going on, it was bad. The streets were deserted; people were huddling indoors for safety. The smell of smoke was everywhere.

IV. TWO MONTHS AGO

No chess game is ever over if the mage piece is still in play.

— Anonymous

In one corner of the Phoenix Guard's grass-covered training field, Lydio Malik ran through his practice routines by himself, as always. Thrust, parry an imaginary foe's counterstrike, sweep left with the heavy, steel practice blade, twice the weight of his issued sword, then dart right, pivot, and begin a new sequence of moves, as if deadly, invisible enemies surrounded him.

Which wasn't far from the truth, sadly.

Despite the summer heat, Malik practiced in full gear, with the heaviest, and dullest, practice sword he could convince a blacksmith to make for him. Full gear included studded leather armor over a padded tunic, his sword, durable black leggings, and an assortment of knives tucked away in different places. He was more lightly armored than most of the other guardsmen, and certainly less well dressed than many, but he preferred to be as unencumbered as possible. He figured speed was his biggest advantage against foes in most fights he could imagine being involved in as a guardsman.

Pivoting, he did another sweep with the blade, when he spotted Gaston Hundersen standing a safe, carefully calculated distance away. Malik stopped, breathing heavily from the exertion, lowered his sword, and said, "What do you want, Gaston?" His fellow guardsman was not a friend, although, in fairness, he didn't routinely belittle Malik for his Neferian heritage as most of the others did.

Malik glanced around, noticing that all the other guardsmen had stopped what they were doing, and were watching them from a distance. Not a good sign.

"Captain Davani wants to see you in his office." Gaston spat on the ground. "I don't think it's good news. I was you, I'd pack my bags afore you go see him." He looked at Malik disdainfully. "And maybe wash up, too."

Without a word, Malik nodded at Gaston, sheathed his practice sword, and walked off the field. As he passed a few of the other guardsmen, one of them said, "Bye, bye, Malik." There was widespread laughter, then another piped up. "Hey, Lydio, I hear they're looking for a bouncer at the Drunken Otter."

He ignored them, just as he ignored all their petty little harassments, racial epithets, and the myriad other ways they expressed their prejudices. He was the first Neferian ever to be selected to the Phoenix Guard, and no matter what happened next, he'd represent his kind with steadfast poise.

Malik headed directly for Davani's office, refusing to cater to the man by washing up first. Let the order's leader see, and smell, what a hard-working guardsman looked like.

That was probably a little unfair to the other guardsmen. Despite their attitude toward him, they were all good, no doubt about that, and they certainly practiced regularly. But it felt to him that most of the men were, at best, simply maintaining their level, content with the skills they'd brought to the Phoenix Guard and unwilling to push harder. Malik blamed Davani for that.

He strode past the barracks and entered the low, stone building beyond it that served as the order's headquarters. Moments later, Davani's administrative adjunct, Delma Sturgsen, a matronly woman who'd grown up in the port city of Cosaturi where Neferians were increasingly common, looked at him with sympathy in her eyes and ushered him into Captain Davani's utilitarian office.

Malik stopped in front of Davani's desk and stood at attention.

Davani ignored him for a moment, his head down as he continued writing on a sheet of paper. Malik recognized petty game-playing when he encountered it and ignored the intentional snub.

Finally, Davani pushed the paper aside, looked up, and said, "At ease."

Malik remained at attention, deliberately, albeit slightly, provoking Davani.

"I'll come straight to the point, Malik," Davani growled. "You're not working out. We're an elite unit and you, quite simply, don't fit in." The gray-haired officer rose to his feet. "The most important thing for our order is teamwork. We work together to serve the royal line. Together." He put his hands down on the desk, leaned over it, and glared at Malik. "Nobody wants to work with you." He opened a drawer, pulled out an official-looking document, and set it on the desk facing Malik. "I want your resignation. Now."

"Permission to speak freely, sir?"

Davani looked at him momentarily, his jaw clenching and unclenching in anger. There were forms that even a commanding officer had to follow. Grudgingly, he said, "Granted."

"I'm not resigning. If you want me gone, then you're going to have to bring charges against me." Malik fixed a level gaze on Davani's face. "I'm prepared to defend myself against any proceeding you may choose to bring."

Davani's face turned red and he angrily slammed his hands down on the desk. He looked as if he was about to shout at Malik, but what came out instead was a much more restrained "Sire," in a surprised voice as the door opened behind Malik and King Salzari strode in, trailed as always by his diminutive secretary, Winton. The King's two bodyguards took up positions outside the door.

"Ah, just the people I was looking for," Salzari said cheerfully. "An opening popped up in my schedule this morning, so I decided to check on our latest recruit." The King turned towards Malik and smiled. Malik noticed his penetrating blue eyes. "Good morning, Lydio Malik. How are you adapting to life as a guardsman?"

"It's been…interesting, Sire."

"Quite. Well, I'm hearing good things about you." Turning back to Davani, he said, "I noticed from your reports that you haven't given Malik an official assignment yet. I rather think he'd be perfectly suited to be Princess Analisa's bodyguard. Her primary, I think."

"But Sire—"

"Make it so," the King said firmly. Without looking again at Malik, he said, "Malik, please find Horatious, my household Chief of Staff, for the particulars of your assignment. You are dismissed."

"Sire," Malik said. He did an about-face and walked past Winton as he exited the office. The mousy-looking secretary fixed his bulging eyes on Malik's face, the left side of his lips quirked upward in an almost imperceptible smile.

Most people dismissed Winton as inconsequential, a servant undeserving of their consideration. Malik suspected that Winton enjoyed being underestimated. He couldn't help but wonder what hand the secretary had played in the King's unexpected visit.

PART II

THE MIDDLE GAME

V. ONE MONTH AGO

Chess is not for timid souls.

— Naryan Svenkali, the Scourge of the North,
  Grand Master, from Neferia

Malik walked through the Hall of Ancestors on his
way to begin his shift protecting Princess Analisa.
Disappointed that Malik hadn't been dismissed from
the order, his fellow guardsmen had begun referring to
his assignment as Diaper Duty, though never in the
hearing of anybody in authority, and calling him the
Nursemaid.

He glanced up at the portraits of twenty-seven
generations of ruling Rukitars, ensconced in their
ornate and gilded frames, as he traversed the dark-
paneled length of the hallway. Five of them had been

assassinated. He liked to think that their spirits sometimes looked out through their portraits, as if they were windows between the spirit realm and the material world, and that they approved of him as a bodyguard. He took his duties seriously. Those five Rukitars who'd died by violence demonstrated that real threats existed. Nothing would ever happen to the princess on his watch, not if he could help it.

Near the end of the hallway, he opened a discreetly unobtrusive servant's door and made his way to the quarters of his royal charge through the maze of plainly decorated servant passages. During the past month, he'd made it his business to learn his way around the palace.

Not just how to get between a few key duty areas, but to learn the palace's halls, passages, and exits like the back of his hand. He'd even sought out the palace mechaneers for further details on the building's layout. With an assignment like his, you never knew when that sort of information might become critical.

Malik opened a door from a servant's passage and walked out into the main hallway of the Royal Wing. A moment later, he knocked on the ornately carved door of the chamber of his royal ward. It opened immediately, revealing Ronston Hardasi, a fellow guardsman. Beyond him, he saw Queen Andu tar Kadafi Rukitar hand her baby, Princess Analisa, to the nursemaid. The queen was conversing with Tulis Razmar, an envoy from the Burgundars, who were allies and close personal friends from Lantille in the north.

Malik made a point of trying to know as much as possible about the people allowed into close proximity to members of the royal family. He'd recognized Razmar from a reception the night before, where he'd quickly come to the impression that the impeccably dressed envoy had an exaggerated sense of his own importance.

Focusing his attention back on Hardasi, Malik couldn't help but notice that the guardsman was holding the door open with his sword hand. He said mildly, "You know, if I'd been an assassin, you'd be dead already." He didn't think guardsmen should even open doors; they should hang back to deal with any threat that might come through a door.

Still in conversation, the queen turned and headed for the exit, Razmar falling a pace behind as dictated by court protocol. Hardasi and Malik stepped out of the way to let the queen and her guest pass between them.

Razmar stopped to look at Malik. "Seriously, assassins?" Shaking his head, he said, "We're in the middle of the royal palace. How would an assassin even get to us here?" Apparently, Razmar had excellent hearing; Malik hadn't intended his comment for anybody but his fellow guardsman.

The queen turned back toward them, laughing, her raven tresses shaking with her merriment. Smiling, the young queen said, "I confess, Malik may be a little paranoid, but I suspect there's no better guardian for my baby." There was an edge to her statement that shut Razmar up.

Hardasi waited until the queen and her guest had progressed some distance down the corridor before he stepped out of the way to let Malik enter the room. "Good news, by the way," he said conspiratorially. "I think you're just in time for her majesty's diaper change." Without any further words, Hardasi left the room.

Melly Scarp, the nursemaid on duty, turned to him. "Hi, Malik," she said cheerfully. "You want to help me change her?"

"Melly, I'm a trained killer. My job is to kill anybody who might try to harm our little princess, not to change diapers."

"Well, you might as well watch and see how it's done. You never know when what you learn might come in handy."

Malik looked down at the princess, all of four months old and fussing because of her messy diaper. Melly undid the baby's diaper, just as she decided to discharge a fresh flow of urine. Malik neatly stepped back as the unexpected flow dribbled over the edge of the changing table.

"Nice reflexes."

"We train for situations like this."

"I bet." The maid snorted, laughing heartily. "Why don't you stand over here and distract her while I take care of things."

Malik stepped around Melly so the, ahem, dangerous end was no longer pointing in his direction. Princess Analisa was undeniably cute. She had bright blue eyes, just like her father. She smiled at Malik and made gurgling noises as she saw the guardsman leaning over her.

Melly finished wiping and powdering, then folded on a new cloth diaper. She pinned one side of the diaper, then said, "Drat!"

"What?" Malik turned his head to look at the nursemaid.

"Lost the other pin. I guess I'll just have to tie it."

Melly twisted the two corners that needed to be attached and nimbly tied them together. The effortless way she did it reminded Malik of sailors he'd seen; he realized she had more than a passing facility with nautical knots.

When the princess made another gurgling noise, he held a finger before her face. She grabbed it with both hands. Her tiny, stubby little fingers were a brilliant white against his much darker skin. Still smiling, she pulled his finger towards her mouth.

Malik didn't realize it until later, but that moment when little Analisa had grabbed his finger was when she became his princess. Not just a shape in swaddling clothes, not just a baby needing a diaper change, but his princess.

His.

VI. NOW

You win chess by taking away your opponent's choices,
so that he can only do what you want.

— Lydio Malik, Phoenix Guard, Unranked Player,
from Intus, Salasia

Malik had just finished changing Princess Analisa's
diaper, using up his only replacement, and had his back
turned, when he heard the next fighter climb onto the
roof's edge. He calmly turned and threw the
exceedingly full diaper he'd just removed at the man,
who cursed when it stuck to his armored chest with a
wet thud.

The royal bodyguard stood and charged downward
at the fighter who, thinking he was a safe distance from
Malik, was prying the diaper off with one hand; his

other hand wasn't holding his sword in a good defensive posture, which was always a mistake around someone of Malik's skill level.

The fighter screamed as Malik ran him through, eyes wide in disbelief at how quickly he'd taken a mortal wound. The man dropped his sword to the roof tiles with a clatter and it promptly slid over the edge.

Holding on to his makeshift rope, Malik kicked the fighter in the chest to dislodge his sword from the man's torso. There was a sucking sound and the sword withdrew about a hands-width from the dead warrior's chest.

Malik gritted his teeth. He hated it when his sword got stuck. He kicked the body three more times before his blade came free. Propelled by the last kick, the rebel's body flew backward off the tower, turning a few uncontrolled somersaults before it landed in the courtyard below.

VII. TWO WEEKS AGO

I am convinced, the way one plays chess reflects the player's personality. If something defines his character, then it will also define his way of playing.

— Vladimar Kramner, Grand Master,
   from Rusitania

It was the middle of the night, just after his shift had ended, when Malik walked into the royal kitchen looking for a cold dinner. He'd been on shift in Princess Analisa's quarters through the dinner hour, and his fellow guardsmen hadn't seen fit to ensure a meal was delivered to him. Just another of the petty ways in which they constantly slighted him.

He found the cook, a chubby, bald man named Rinaldo Sigursen, sitting at the kitchen table, looking morosely at a chess set.

"Problems?" Malik asked, gesturing at the board game.

"I've got a bet with Chently, the Queen's butler, that I can beat him in a chess game. He got called away, so we agreed to finish the game in the morning."

Malik scanned the board intently. "How much is the bet?"

"Well, it's only a crown," Rinaldo replied. "But it's the principle of the matter! Chently's insufferable. He's always lording it over the rest of us. I just wanted to take him down a peg." He groaned and put his head in his hands. "I didn't realize he was such a great player."

"You're playing white, I assume?"

"Yes."

"You're down in pieces, but you've got checkmate in seven moves if you execute properly."

"What!" The cook looked up in surprise.

"You win chess by taking away your opponent's choices, so that he can only do what you want." Malik reached down and moved the mage piece. "See, the queen is now in danger. He's got no choice but to protect her, because all of his other choices are worse."

Malik showed Rinaldo the rest of the key moves, as well as Chently's possible responses.

The cook shook his head disbelievingly, studying the changed board. "It seems so simple, now, but I just couldn't see that." He looked up at Malik. "You know, you're all right." He got up from the table. "Let me warm up something for you."

The cook began bustling around the kitchen. Over his shoulder, he said, "I'll get you a good meal, then you're going to have just enough time to pack when you get back to your quarters."

"Come again?"

"Nobody's told you?" Rinaldo turned and looked at Malik in surprise. "You're leaving for Lantille in the morning. The queen and the princess are going to stay in Lantille with the Burgundars, who are old friends of hers. The king will stay for a week, then he's taking a bunch of troops and going further north to show the flag around Karsh."

VIII. NOW

In life, as in chess, forethought wins.

— Cho Sumari, Grand Master, from Hestria

Melly sat on an ornate wooden chair, under the watchful eyes of her two guards, and observed the preparations for the next assault on Malik with a certain amount of fear, as well as curiosity and, perhaps, just a bit of anticipation. So far as she could tell, the royal bodyguard was still ahead in points in this dance of death that Razmar had put in motion. Malik had predicted and prepared for every move made so far by the traitor.

It had taken quite a while for Razmar to cajole two more fighters into agreeing to assault Malik, and neither had been willing to do so without some sort of lifeline. It had taken even more time to track down some ropes.

It was interesting that Pandomar, who seemed to be the leader, or at least the most senior, of the Kashmal fighters, hadn't really helped. *An uneasy alliance*, she thought. She didn't think Pandomar had much respect for Razmar, who came across as something of a manipulative bastard.

The two reluctant volunteers, one tall and lanky and the other stocky but tough-looking, had ropes tied to their waists and attached to a bedpost of a heavy wooden bed that had been pushed up next to the window.

Malik was sat on the tiles just below the royal basket, conserving his energy. When the next fighter climbed to the roof, the man was head and shoulders taller than him, with a scruffy brown beard and shaggy hair. Malik hadn't heard the climber because the Princess kept crying insistently. She was undoubtedly hungry by now.

He noted that the man had a rope tied around his waist. He'd imagined, or at least hoped, that it was getting harder for Razmar to convince his men to climb up and challenge him.

It amused Malik that the rebel fighters were worried enough now that they wanted a safety line in case they fell. From a numbers perspective, given the vicious fight up the tower's stairs and now on the roof, they should be considerably more worried about him than any potential fall. Malik assumed the rope was tied to the bed in the room below. It was the only piece of furniture built solidly enough to serve as an effective anchor.

He rubbed his eyes tiredly and stood up, his joints creaking in protest. He was a body length and a half away from his fresh assailant, who drew a long, narrow sword. Grinning at Malik with crooked yellow teeth, he stepped to the side, and another fighter, shorter, broader, and more heavily muscled, climbed laboriously onto the orange tiles. A rope was tied around his waist as well.

Left hand on his lifeline, Malik drew his sword and descended the slope to dispatch his newest challengers.

As he approached, he exchanged a few quick parries with the lanky fighter, who showed some dueling experience. The stocky fighter drew a shortsword and moved up the slope, trying to circle around Malik so that he and his partner could both attack simultaneously. A dangerous combination.

Malik dropped to the tiles on his back, sliding downward, which put him into the position he wanted. He kicked the lanky fighter in the kneecap. The fighter yelled in pain, lost his balance, and tumbled backward off the roof.

The stocky fighter charged forward and thrust his sword at Malik in an attempt to run him through.

The blow never landed.

There was an audible thud as the falling fighter hit the end of the rope, then a loud cracking sound from the room below as the bed broke apart where Malik and Melly had weakened it during their siege preparations. The pieces of the broken bed joined the first fighter in his uncontrolled plummet. The combined weight suddenly hit the remaining fighter as he was tried to step forward, slamming him face-first into the tiles and then yanking him off the roof before he realized what had happened.

Malik smiled as he heard cursing from the room below. *You take away your enemy's choices so he does what you want*, he thought.

As he stood up, something slammed into the side of his head, slicing from his forehead just above his right eye and all the way to his ear. He realized almost instantly that he'd just been hit with a glancing arrow shot. He threw himself back down on the tiles and tried to roll out of range of the south tower, the only tower the enemy could have used to target him. He almost made it to safety, but couldn't help screaming in agony as an arrow lodged solidly in his arm.

His sword arm.

While Razmar cursed uncontrollably, Melly watched as Pandomar stared for a long moment at the remains of the shattered bed lying beneath the window. He turned his head, fixed his gaze on Melly, and said, "You knew?"

"Of course," Melly replied, smiling brightly. "Who do you think sawed the bed in pieces?"

The fighters in the room glared at her now with tangible animosity. Melly felt her survival balanced on a knife edge. Even Razmar stopped cursing to pay attention to them.

"The sawdust went out the window, I assume?"

"Yes."

"And cutting the sheets into strips and making ropes of them?"

"My father was a sailor on the River Gahtani. He taught me knots."

Melly was so focused on Pandomar that she was surprised when Razmar started laughing. She could tell that Pandomar and his Kashmal warriors were not amused as they withdrew their attention from her and glowered at him.

"Clever, my dear. Very clever." Razmar turned towards the warriors. "Let that be a lesson to you, men, she doesn't even have any weapons, and she's still managed to kill two of you. Face it, you've been beaten by the nanny." He shook his head, still laughing.

"Well," Pandomar said, "we'd be gone by now if you hadn't gotten your mage killed."

Razmar shrugged. "I had no way of knowing that the Queen's butler was a mage. At least he's dead, too." He smiled at Pandomar, but there was nothing friendly about it. "Meanwhile, the vaunted Kashmal warriors, the terror of the mountains, the scourge of the valleys, can't even finish off a single injured man."

That was news to Melly. She'd had no idea Chently was a mage, either, and she'd known him for years.

Pandomar scowled and stepped forward. "We'll get him."

"I hope so," Razmar said glibly. "There must be some reason for us to be allied with your tribes. Right now, I'm having trouble figuring out what it is." He turned towards Melly. "Do you have any more surprises for us?"

"Um, no. I'm done," she said.

Well, that was only sort of true, Melly thought. It was a dangerous game Malik was playing up there on the roof. But she didn't think Razmar knew the game had a well-defined time limit. It wasn't common knowledge, but she knew that the Queen used some sort of magical artifact to communicate with the King every morning and every evening. She didn't think that Razmar knew this, so it had just been dumb luck that his attack had occurred shortly after the morning communication. Missing the evening contact, though, was going to be noticed.

If Malik could stay alive until sunset, well, then they might all have a chance to survive. By her estimation, it was an hour past the noon hour. Malik needed to survive about another four hours.

She studied Pandomar thoughtfully, unsure why he hadn't killed her yet. He was stoic as Razmar berated the tribal fighters, finally demanding that two men be sent downstairs to retrieve the ropes.

Danteel sat in a wooden chair next to one of his shop's shuttered windows, periodically peeking through an observation hole at the empty streets. He was wearing his sword for the first time since his brief stint in the militia fifteen years before. A prudent man carried a sword in times of trouble, no matter how out of practice he might be with it. Still, once trained, always trained, as one of his long-ago weapon instructors had said.

His wife had fixed him a cold lunch, which now rested like an uncomfortable lump in his stomach. She was upstairs with the younger children, while he waited for either Chanama to return or for some enterprising soul to take advantage of the situation to rob his store.

He heard footsteps on the wooden walkway outside, which he'd built so that his more genteel customers didn't have to worry about mud and other sundry substances when they alighted from their fancy carriages.

He stood up, hand on sword, then relaxed as he recognized the familiar pattern of the family knock on the door.

Danteel strode to the door, unlatched it, and peered through the gap. Chanama stood outside, tall and gangly like a colt.

"Pa—"

"Get inside, boy." He quickly ushered his son inside and latched the door again. "Thought you'd hunker down for the duration."

His son stared at the sheathed sword hanging at Danteel's belt, something he'd never seen him wearing before.

"I did," the boy said. "But the Market's on fire…most of the waterfront's on fire. I had to move when it started coming my way."

"All right." Danteel nodded. "When trouble comes, you make the best decisions you can. You did well. Good to see you safe and sound."

"I saw something weird on the way, Pa. I think somebody's fighting on the roof of the north tower."

IX. FIVE DAYS AGO

Chess is a waste of time, an outmoded hobby from a past era, of interest only to imbeciles, the elderly, and other useless layabouts.

— Tulis Razmar, Revolutionary, from Lantille, Salasia

Malik strode up to the group of ten servants surrounding Angston Malde, the Burgundar's liaison with the Queen's security forces. Malde was a thin, balding man in his late fifties who looked dapper in what Malik recognized as the latest court style. The liaison glanced up at him, but continued to pass out instructions to the servants. All of his orders seemed to address minutiae associated with court etiquette and precedence.

Malik waited patiently for Malde to finish. After listening for a few minutes, he came to three conclusions. First, Malde liked to lord it over the other servants. Second, he was ignoring Malik. And finally, he didn't seem to have the same grasp of court precedence as Malik.

"Excuse me," Malik said. "I have a few questions…"

Malde said sharply, "I've already spoken to your senior officers. All necessary security arrangements have been made."

"Well, I still have some things I need to know."

"Sir," Malde said haughtily, "that is not my problem." He turned away from Malik to speak to another servant.

Malik reached out with both hands and gently pushed the two closest servants aside as he stepped between them. He dropped his hand heavily on the liaison's shoulder and spun him around. The functionary's mouth opened wide with surprise. Malik grabbed him by the throat with his right hand and lifted him into the air. He took four more steps to the left and slammed Malde's back into the wall, his feet dangling two feet off the floor. He held the man at arms-length with no visible strain.

In a soft, calm voice, he said, "I am the primary bodyguard for the princess. If I have questions about her safety, there is nothing more important in your life. Do you understand me?"

Malde moved his head up and down ever so slightly, which was about all the mobility that he had left with Malik holding him up by his throat. The bodyguard let him go; the functionary fell to the floor and slid to a sitting position. Holding his throat, he gasped for breath.

Malik turned to the servants. "Leave us."

The servants obediently scurried away.

Malik squatted next to the liaison. "I don't care what you've discussed with the rest of the Queen's security forces. I do things my way.

"So, I want to understand the layout of this entire castle. If you have plans or drawings, I need to see them. I want to know about any nooks, crannies, hidden features, and possible escape routes. I want to see the towers. I want to see the lowest levels. I want to see the private areas. By the end of the day, I will know this castle like the back of my own hand, or I will pitch your worthless carcass from the highest window of the tallest tower."

X. NOW

It is not a move, even the best move that
you must seek, but a realizable plan.

— Yevgen Borovsky, Grand Master, from Rusitania

Malik sat on the roof just below the princess's basket, safely out of sight of the archers in the south tower, and waited for the next development. He'd achieved an almost meditative state, ignoring the pain of his various wounds, impending exhaustion, and thirst. His sword arm, now bandaged with a strip of cloth cut from the princess's blanket, was all but useless; he couldn't hold his sword in his right hand anymore.

He'd trained left-handed for just this type of eventuality, but no master swordsman was ever equally proficient with both hands. Never in his wildest dreams had he ever expected to really have to fight any adversaries with his off hand.

Now his life, and the life of his princess, depended on it.

He'd moved his sword's sheath to his right side so he could draw his sword cross-body with his left hand. He held his favorite dagger in his left hand. It had been a gift from the legion when he'd left the service. His men had told him that he'd clearly need something to cut his meat with when he left, especially since he was getting "a little long in the tooth." Then they'd handed him an excellent Sarakanth blade, razor sharp and perfectly balanced for throwing.

Malik heard sounds from the other side of the roof, the dangerous side that was under the watchful eye of the enemy archers in the south tower. He recognized the sounds of someone climbing onto the roof. After a moment, he was able to determine that multiple men had just climbed onto the roof.

They would probably split up—send one around the spire to take him from behind.

He stood up slowly. It was time for some more edgework.

He turned around to wrap a little bit more of his knotted lifeline around his waist. When the makeshift rope was suitably taut, he charged forward, the rope drawing him into a circular path around the roof's spire.

As he rounded the roof, he saw three fighters arrayed in front of him, all with ropes tied around their waists. He threw his dagger at the second fighter and saw it sink with a meaty thunk into the man's throat. Still running at full speed, he drew his sword in a flashing arc that parried the closest fighter's blade and knocked it to the side. He slammed his shoulder into the man and knocked him backward off the roof.

The third man tried to run him through, but misjudged his strike as Malik's anchoring rope turned his running path into an arc. With the fighter's sword out of any realistic defensive position, Malik cut his throat as he sprinted by, blood spraying into the afternoon air.

Malik continued running and managed to circumnavigate the entire roof so quickly that he was able to get back to the relative safety of his side before the shocked archers managed to get off a shot. Hidden from their view, they never saw how his injured leg finally buckled underneath him, throwing him heavily to the tiles on top of his damaged right arm. They never saw how stunned he was by the impact, how helpless he was for the next five minutes or how he could barely stand once he finally managed to get to his feet again.

XI. FOUR HOURS AGO

In master-level chess, you have to drive
your advantage home unmercifully.

— Fisher Kozen, Grand Master, from Malawi

Melly clutched Princess Analisa's basket to her chest and ran as fast as she could in the wake of Ronston Hardasi, the bodyguard on duty when the attack started. He led them down a narrow, marble-lined hallway in a seldom-used section of the fortress, desperately looking for an escape route that wasn't blocked by enemy forces. His bloody sword was out; he'd already had to cut his way past a few attackers. She couldn't help wishing Malik was here; he'd know what to do.

Hardasi stopped suddenly as six enemy fighters rounded the corner up ahead. To Melly's eyes, they looked like Kashmal tribal warriors, which wasn't much of a surprise. They were at the bottom of most of the unrest in the north. The surprise, of course, was that they were here right now in what King Salzari had considered a safe bastion for his family.

There was a momentary tableau as the two sides considered each other. Melly saw smiles appear on the faces of the fighters as they realized the import of the basket that Melly was carrying. She surmised that there were probably bonuses, or at least bragging rights, for any fighter that managed to kill the queen or the princess. She wondered if they realized the kind of wrath Salzari would unleash upon the north after today.

The warriors charged and Hardasi met them with a whirling storm of steel, one expert swordsman against six seasoned and well-armored opponents.

Melly could see that it wasn't going to be enough. Hardasi was good, but he was far too outnumbered. She put down the basket and grabbed an unlit torch from a wall sconce. It was the best weapon she could improvise.

To his credit, Hardasi managed to kill two of them and injure two more before they finally got him. He fell to his knees, impaled by a sword, the point sticking wetly out of his back. He dropped his sword on the stone floor with a metallic clatter.

A bearded warrior planted his boot on Hardasi's chest and pushed until his sword came out with a sickening squelch. As Hardasi's body fell to the side, the four remaining warriors advanced, grinning mercilessly.

Somewhere behind them, Melly heard a door open and she saw three of the warriors turn to face the other direction. Suddenly Malik was there, like some magical demigod of death and mayhem. It was as if the warriors were standing still. His sword licked out, bypassing parries and finding weak points in armor. He slaughtered them in under five seconds, the first still falling to the floor as he thrust his sword through the throat of the last.

"All of the planned escape routes are blocked," Malik said, casually wiping his sword on the fur coat of one of the warriors.

"What are we going to do, then?" Melly asked, strangely calm despite all the bloodshed.

"We're going to the north tower. If they want us, they'll have to pay the price in blood." Malik grinned and added, "More blood than they ever expected."

XII. NOW

Never underestimate the power of a pawn.

— Karkomir, Grand Master, from Salasia

Malik lay on the tiles next to the princess. Smiling, he sang her a lullaby in a rough, untrained voice, the rhythmic banging from below providing the beat for the melody. The princess began fussing again, albeit weakly. Malik was happy to see that she was still all right.

He'd pulled himself up to her level because he wanted to see her face one more time before he died. Survival had always been a long shot, but now he could sense even the possibility receding. Between his injuries, blood loss, almost unbearable thirst, and exhaustion from the day's extreme exertions, he just didn't have much left. He couldn't even feel his right arm anymore. Every other part of his body ached, and he was still slowly losing blood from some of his wounds.

Beneath him, his enemies were trying to dismantle the roof so they could get at them more easily. He'd been told the roof and supporting structure were ironwood, though, which explained why the tower could have such a flat slope for so much of the roof, even in the north where snow was so prevalent.

The princess turned her head toward him, whimpering despite his tune. Her blue eyes glittered in the afternoon sun. She was beautiful.

His princess.

His.

PART III

The Endgame

XIII. NOW AND THEN

You have to have the fighting spirit. You have to force moves and take chances.

— Fisher Kozen, Grand Master, from Malawi

Melly had decided that the only reason she was still alive was because Razmar was a show-off. He enjoyed demonstrating his power in front of others, and she was the only available audience. Plus, under the pretense of talking to her, he could disparage his Kashmal partners. She could see that Pandomar was seething with anger, as were his men. She suspected it was only Pandomar's oath to his clan leader that kept him from killing Razmar himself, and, in turn, he was all that kept his warriors in check.

However, Razmar wasn't unintelligent. His superior attitude and constant needling were carefully calculated. He knew there was a limit to how far he could go, but he enjoyed pushing close to that limit.

Surprisingly, while it was true that Razmar would never be liked or respected as a leader, his tactics were highly effective at spurring his Kashmal compatriots in their labors. She suspected he was a highly proficient merchant.

He should have stuck to business. Salzari was going to kill him when he caught the traitor. Slowly and painfully.

There was a loud *clunk* as a hammer fell to the floor from the hole that Pandomar's men had ripped into the ceiling. Melly was just thankful that the banging had finally stopped.

A stocky man stuck his head out of the hole and looked down at them. He had a wrinkled face surrounded by a halo comprised almost equally of long dark hair and a bushy beard shot through with gray. "Sorry about that, it slipped," he called out. "It don't matter, though. It's all ironwood. Every single strut and every single roof board. Can't even imagine how much this gods-be-damned tower must've cost."

"What about the nails?" Pandomar asked.

"It's mage-built. Every single damned nail's been driven at least a half-inch deep, and then covered with filler. You'd have to find each nail, so's we'd need more light up here. Then you'd have to chisel down to the head of each nail afore you could even try getting it out. I'd estimate an hour per nail, eight nails to a roof board.

"You'd need to take out two roof boards afore you'd get a man through them, and then that devil Malik would just be there with his sword."

"How about if we had men working in parallel?" Razmar said.

"Para what?" The man looked doubtful.

Razmar scowled. "If we had multiple men working on nails at the same time."

The man looked up and away from the watchers below, clearly studying the construction and the web of struts supporting the roof. Looking down again, he said, "Four men at once, perched on the supports, two on each board. So you're looking at maybe four hours to make a man-size opening."

Pandomar and Razmar both cursed at the same time, then eyed each other sheepishly.

Razmar called up, " How about burning the roof?"

"Hellfire, man, you ever tried to burn ironwood?" The man chuckled.

"No."

"It burns, but you gots to get it ferociously hot afore it catches. And even then, it takes hours and hours to burn through. You're better off prying out nails than trying to burn ironwood."

Razmar thought a moment. Then he grinned evilly. "I have an idea," he said. "Two ideas, actually."

The warriors in the room stared at him balefully. They'd already learned to be leery of his ideas.

Lydio Malik clutched his father's hand as they walked down the...well, he wasn't sure what the street was really called, so he just called it the Street With All the Statues. Intus was like nothing Lydio had ever seen, and he was almost six years old. There were so many people, dressed in so many different ways, and speaking languages he'd never heard before. Everything was so much larger than the farming village where he lived with his family.

Some soldiers in polished armor came along, shouting, "Make way, make way!" All of the people shuffled to the sides of the road. His father lifted him onto his shoulders so he could see better.

A group of soldiers marched past them, the beat of their boots echoing off the buildings. Lydio thought they looked really dangerous, like nobody would ever mess with them, unlike the other boys in the village who picked on him because of his dark skin. There was a gap and then another group of soldiers marched by, and Lydio thought they looked way more dangerous than the first ones. They were wearing black armor with gold trim.

"Look at the sojers, Daddy," Lydio exclaimed. "How come they have black armor?"

"Those are the Phoenix Guards, boy. Must be royalty coming down the street."

"Are they really, really dangerous?"

"Son, they're the toughest fighters around," his father said. "They're elite, so elite that there's only ever two hundred of them."

"I wanna be a Phoenix Guard!"

His father laughed. "You can't, son, they'll never take a Neferian, no matter how good he is." It was years before he understood the bitterness behind his father's laughter.

The Phoenix Guards moved past but the banging sound of their boots didn't go away. Then he realized he was dreaming, lost in a childhood memory, but the banging was real. He wondered what his enemies had been up to while he'd been lost in a stupor.

His thoughts were muddled, fuzzy from fatigue, but he nevertheless tried to reason out what their next move could be. Dismantling the roof wasn't going to work for them, not in the timeframe they needed. He had the sense that the banging had stopped for a while, and then restarted while he was dreaming. Why had it stopped?

Because they'd realized they couldn't get through the roof quickly.

Why start up again?

A distraction?

Had he been in their place, he'd up the ante. Hit him with multiple attacks at the same time.

If he were going to do that, some sort of distraction would be helpful—a distraction like the continued banging from underneath the roof.

He sighed. Letting the knotted rope slide through his left hand, he started to lower himself down the relatively steep slope of the roof, where he'd been resting next to the princess. As he did so, he caught

67

sight of something—a jug of some kind—arcing through the air. It shattered on the tiles just below him and a clear liquid splashed out.

He had a feeling it wasn't water. Probably oil.

Malik desperately scrabbled with his feet, first to avoid sliding down into the oil. And second, to get back up to the princess before his assailants pitched the next oil-filled container at them.

And there it was…another ceramic jug. Malik reached up and batted it aside. It landed with a crash on the lower part of the roof.

Another one sailed overhead, aimed in a high arc at the spire above the princess, but the thrower's aim was bad. It sailed over Malik and the princess and landed with a crash in almost the same spot as the one Malik had diverted.

A fourth jug sailed through the air on an almost perfect trajectory for the princess. Malik lunged upward, got his hand on it, and reeled it in to his chest, unbroken.

He quickly tucked it into the foot of the princess's basket; anything you had that the enemy didn't know you had was a potential advantage.

He heard more ceramic breaking from the other side of the roof. The banging was continuing from below, so it was hard to be sure what he was hearing from the other side, but he was pretty sure the jug throwers were abandoning their position on the roof. He was certain he knew what was going to happen next.

The princess cried weakly, disturbed by all the noise. He wrapped the knotted rope around his left arm and then, with the limited mobility available to him in his precariously angled position, he pulled Princess Analisa's dainty, frilly little blouse up to cover her nose and mouth. He took her blanket and wrapped it around the bottom portion of his own face.

He heard the sound of something striking the other side of the roof, a flaming arrow, most likely. There's was a whooshing sound as the oil on the other side of the roof caught fire. Then tendrils of flame raced across to their side. Larger fires started where the oil jugs had broken on the tiles. Gray smoke billowed into the air and enveloped them.

Danteel had an advantage over his neighbors. Most of the buildings around his shop were only two stories tall, so the windows on his third floor gave him a good view of the city. In fact, only the Teradawn clan, with their ancient, upgraded four-story tenement, possessed a better vantage. Of course, that was mainly because they were even closer to Paksenaral, which gave them more elevation.

Danteel and his hulking friend, Orlik, were discussing the Situation, while Chanama took a turn looking out the third-floor window at the north tower with a sleek-looking farlooker, a mechanical device that enhanced vision. It was an awkward device, but exceedingly useful.

The silversmith had ventured out and found Orlik, a fellow shopkeeper with whom he'd served in the militia. As a fourth-generation weapon smith, Orlik had always been fascinated by gadgets. Living up to his military reputation as a scrounger, he'd "liberated" a farlooker when he and Danteel had mustered out.

So far, they'd ascertained that Chanama had been right about fighting on the north tower's roof. There was indeed a man on the roof, and he was defending what looked like a baby basket that was somehow tied to the roof's spire. And he was wearing colors that Danteel and Orlik recognized as belonging to the Phoenix Guard. He could only think of one baby that the Phoenix Guard would be trying so desperately to protect.

Now they were trying to burn that lone guardsman out.

"It has to be Princess Analisa," Danteel said.

"Yeah."

"It's got to be a small force," Danteel mused. "There's no army roaming the streets, pillaging."

Orlik grunted. "So they smashed the militia by surprise, caused havoc by burning everything in sight…"

"Then punched out the fortress garrison."

"Pa," Chanama interjected. "There's some men coming out the front gate."

"Let me see," Danteel responded. His son handed him the farlooker.

Danteel leaned over the boy and focused on the front gate. A team of eight men, attired like Kashmal warriors, was moving quickly through the streets. Two of them carried bows.

He handed the farlooker to Orlik, who grunted.

"I won't stand for it," Danteel said, standing up tall. "Once trained, always trained."

"I'm in," Orlik said.

XIV. NOW

It's always better to sacrifice your opponent's men.

— Samiel Tartak, Grand Master, from Antellum

The fires had died out and a mild afternoon breeze was gradually clearing the smoke away, but Malik couldn't stop coughing. The blanket had helped, but he'd nevertheless inhaled a lot of smoke.

Still, there really wasn't anything to burn on the roof except the oil itself. Now that the flames were gone, he expected the next attack at any moment.

He was right about the imminent attack, but not its direction of approach. Still coughing and spitting phlegm out of his mouth, he just barely caught a glimpse of something flashing through the air. An arrow struck the tile next to the royal basket and ricocheted away. He tried to backtrack its trajectory from his brief glimpse and realized that his enemies had placed an archer outside the castle. Probably in that tall building that the Burgundars should never have allowed so close to the fortress.

He tried to judge the arrow shot critically. The four-story building was downhill from the fortress. The distance was long and the elevation difference was extreme. It took an excellent archer, a seriously powerful archer, to get an arrow up here. But it took time, precious time, for an arrow to traverse that kind of distance. At least two whole seconds in flight, with an extreme arc to get it on target.

Malik quickly struggled to his feet, standing outward at an angle supported only by his lifeline, and positioned himself between the archer and the princess.

He spotted another arrow arcing in their direction and managed to knock it aside with his sword. He suddenly doubled over, coughing uncontrollably, and missed the next one. He and the princess lucked out as it flew harmlessly past. He diverted two more arrows, but then one came in too low for him to effectively reach. Or maybe he was slowing down.

He screamed as it drove into his lower right leg and lodged solidly into bone. His leg buckled underneath him, but he managed to assume a kneeling position that still kept his body between the princess and the archer.

The arrows stopped. Despite his fatigue, Malik was still alert enough to recognize this as yet another bad sign. A moment later, a single fighter, rope tied to his waist, stepped carefully into view, careful of his balance and avoiding the still smoldering pools where the oil had burned. His sword was held quite properly in a guard position.

"Hoy, Malik!" he called. "Having a bit of trouble, eh?" The man had an erect, confident carriage. He wore a fine set of half-and-half armor, heavy leather with a chain mail insert covering his torso—less than half the weight and better mobility than chain mail, but more protection than leather armor in most fighting situations. He moved easily, gracefully. Malik decided he was the most dangerous opponent they'd sent up yet. If he was alone, it was because he didn't want any interference.

"You got a name?" Malik said, using his one good leg to lift himself into a standing position. His arrow-shot leg, the arrow still protruding, protested every movement.

The fighter looked up at Malik, ten feet away and perhaps eight feet higher, and laughed. "Nakanti, son of Pandomar, hero of Antigon, and, soon enough, the slayer of the Royal Bodyguard."

"Well, that hero thing is kind of dubious, seeing as how your side not only lost but got horsewhipped all the way back to your caves in the mountains." Malik saw the man's face flush with anger; he'd all but called

Nakanti a savage, an uncouth cave dweller. "And the slayer part, I think I object to that."

"Well, come on down and let us do the dance of steel, that we may decide the issue."

Malik reached into the princess's basket, ignoring the protests from his bad leg, lifted the jug of oil, and smashed it on the tiles a few feet in front of Nakanti, splashing him with oil.

Nakanti jumped to the side, landing in a spot untouched by oil from this or any of the previous jugs. Oil from the new jug ignited when several narrow streams reached still smoldering patches. Unfortunately, Nakanti was untouched.

"Tricky," the fighter said. "But your tricks won't save you now."

Orlik led the way down a narrow alley, massive war axe in hand, followed by Danteel. Orlik's oldest son, Miska, already the biggest man among all of them at nineteen, carrying a heavy-weight bow, came next, and eight other locals that Danteel had quickly recruited. They made a motley procession, but they all shared a determination to do something about the Situation. None of them could stand by and let the princess be slaughtered. Maybe they couldn't take back the fortress, but they could damn well take out the archers their enemies had sent out to get a new angle on the lone rooftop defender.

They were all armed with weapons from Orlik's shop. The bulky weapon smith hadn't hesitated for a moment at arming his fellow volunteers. Most of them even had some experience using them, thanks to mandatory militia service during previous conflicts with the Kashmal.

As they reached the final corner, Danteel called a halt. Then he peeked around the corner at the Teradawn tenement.

He turned and said quietly to the men, "Door's been smashed open. If these buggers have any brains, they'll have left at least one guard in the foyer."

Orlik rumbled, "You've been here before, I take it?"

"Yeah. There's a stairway on the left. If a guard gets up the stairs, our job gets harder. Much harder."

"All right," Orlik said. "We go in fast, two on each side of the entrance, Miska down the center with the bow. Two on the left, enter and then wait to see what has to happen, 'cause Miska's going to cover the stairs with his bow, and you ain't getting in his way if you know what's good for you."

Orlik picked three men to join him and Miska on the initial assault, leaving Danteel to lead the remaining men in behind them. One of the volunteers who hadn't been chosen for the initial strike complained, "Hey, I want to fight, too."

Danteel chuckled. He pointed at Orlik's little team as they assembled at the corner. "They're Shock. The rest of us, we're Awe."

"What's that mean?" the volunteer asked.

"They see Orlik and company, they're shocked," Danteel said.

Orlik turned and added, "They see the rest of you guys, they go—'Awww…we're so screwed.'"

The men chuckled. A moment later, Orlik led his assault team around the corner.

XV. NOW

The winner of the game is the one who makes the next-to-last mistake.

—— Samiel Tartak, Grand Master, from Antellum

Malik was surprised that Nakanti waited patiently for him to come down to a fighting position lower on the roof. He thought about leaping from above and various other stratagems, but decided that Nakanti was too good a swordsman for such maneuvers to work. So he descended laboriously, unwrapping the lifeline from his arm and half-hopping on his one good leg. He tried to fake being worse off than he really was, but there wasn't much room to fake being worse off.

The Kashmal warrior waited until Malik caught his breath from the laborious climb down, then inquired politely, "Are you ready now? I can give you a little more time if you'd like."

Malik raised an eyebrow. "You worried about my health?"

"You have fought valiantly. I can't help but regret the passing of such a mighty warrior." He paused. "But rejoice to know that your name will forever take pride of place in the songs they shall sing of my accomplishments."

Malik gave him an incredulous look, then shook his head tiredly. "Let's get it over with."

Their swords clanged and slid against each other in an intricate series of strikes as they tested each other's skills. They were both hampered a little, Malik by his immobility and Nakanti by his desire to avoid some of the still-burning patches and rivulets of oil. Malik would have been by far the better swordsman under normal circumstances. As it was, Nakanti clearly had the edge—younger, faster, fresher, and uninjured.

Nakanti suddenly darted up the slope, higher than Malik could reach with his sword, but instead of going after the princess, the younger fighter wheeled, drew his sword along Malik's taut lifeline, and cut it asunder.

Malik figured out what Nakanti was doing just barely in time to brace himself, so he staggered but didn't fall. He could feel his legs shaking with strain.

Nakanti laughed and, still keeping a safe distance from Malik, pretended to saunter casually as he descended the slope back to Malik's level.

Malik said, "Well, you've cut my rope. If you're going to play fair, you should get rid of your rope, too."

"You're welcome to try to cut it yourself." Nakanti grinned, showing off his white, slightly uneven teeth. "If you can."

The warrior circled around Malik, testing the bodyguard's defenses, carefully aware of his footwork to avoid tripping on the edges of the tiles or stepping in any of the oil. His moves gradually got more aggressive as he pressed Malik harder. Worn down as he was, Malik had an increasingly difficult time parrying his thrusts.

Malik had realized one thing, though. Nakanti had probably never fought anybody of Malik's caliber before. He didn't realize that there was a slight predictability to his moves. Malik waited for Nakanti to make the right move.

The bodyguard recognized the minute stance change that heralded Nakanti's next thrust. Instead of blocking it, he deliberately stepped forward and drove his right shoulder into Nakanti's blade, trapping it in his own flesh. Malik roared with the pain, but still managed a descending swing that took out the younger man's throat in a wash of blood.

His sword clanged down to the tiles and wedged there as Nakanti fell on top of it. Then Malik slipped and fell on top of him. There was a snapping sound as Malik's sword shattered; he saw the middle piece of it arcing through the air.

Then he and Nakanti were tumbling. He dropped what remained of his sword and scrabbled against the tiles, breaking his fingernails, to try to keep himself from going over the edge. Somewhere in that mad rolling, Nakanti's blade came out of his shoulder, adding a whole new dimension of pain to Malik's experience. He just managed to slow himself in time as the fighter and his blade sailed into the abyss. When he stopped, both his legs from the thigh down were hanging in the open air.

Malik carefully shimmied his way fully back onto the roof. The pommel of his sword was still attached to his left wrist, along with eight inches of the shattered blade.

Melly saw the rope go taut as Nakanti fell off the roof and knew Malik had managed to kill yet another attacker. Only one person had been knocked off the roof and lived, and he had steadfastly refused to go back up and face the "demon" again. She suspected that Nakanti was the best fighter they'd sent up so far, too good to be shouldered over the edge like the one survivor.

She felt a brief twinge of sorrow. Nakanti had been kind to her. Under other circumstances, she could have even liked him. This was tempered by her elation at knowing that Malik, and the princess, were both still alive.

She heard Razmar by the window cursing and making disparaging remarks about the tribal warriors. She looked up a Pandomar, who was standing near her, and saw his face tighten as he realized that his son was gone. His face flushed with anger at Razmar's comments, but he visibly controlled himself.

"I'm sorry for your loss," Melly said.

Pandomar fixed his penetrating gaze on her face. He grunted, then nodded almost imperceptibly as he realized she was serious. He turned to watch as three of his men grabbed the rope and began the laborious task of hauling Nakanti's body up to the window.

One of the men suddenly screamed and fell backward, clutching an arrow that had sprouted from his chest. The other two men dropped the rope and leapt away from the window.

Melly took this as a good omen. Someone was trying to help them. She struggled not to smile, since antagonizing her captors wasn't exactly in her best interests.

"Ser Razmar," Pandomar said drily. "I believe we have a new player in your little game."

"We're not leaving until the princess is dead." Razmar looked around haughtily. "If your paper warriors could just do their job, we'd already be out of here."

The Karshmen in the room glared at Razmar, except for Pandomar, who was utterly still. Melly wondered if Razmar knew how close Pandomar was to just killing him and leaving.

After a long moment, Pandomar pointed to one of his men. "Tell the archers in the south tower to kill whoever's shooting at us." The man started walking to the door. "Run!" Pandomar roared, spurring the fighter to sprint out of the room.

Time dragged by as the opposing archers fought their slow-paced, long-range duel. While the struggle continued, Pandomar's men managed to raise Nakanti's body without exposing themselves to arrow fire. Pandomar had his son's body placed on what remained of the bed, now pushed up against the far wall. Nakanti looked almost like he was resting in state.

From what Melly overheard during the struggle, it was clear that the opposing archer was part of a group that had forcibly replaced the team Razmar had placed outside the fortress. The archer was also acting strategically, suppressing the rebels' capability to get to the roof rather than trying to inflict damage. Melly suspected that her unlikely ally might also be conserving arrows.

Razmar pushed for another team to be sent to take out their opposition, but Pandomar summarily rejected the suggestion. By then, someone had organized the locals and there were hundreds of hostile citizens in the streets, many of them armed with makeshift weapons, all focused on the drama of the north tower stand-off. Instead, Pandomar pre-staged three fighters with ropes, so they could go on the attack as soon as it was safe again.

Melly heard someone running up the stairs, then one of the younger warriors burst into the room and shouted, "They got him! They got him!"

She felt a pang of sorrow for the unknown archer. Still, by her estimate, whoever it was had cost Razmar and Pandomar more than an hour, maybe even an hour and a half, of precious time.

XVI. NOW

Tactics means doing what you can with what you have.

— Alina Skye, Mercenary Commander

Malik was lying down and resting. Well, actually, he wasn't entirely sure he could stand up again. He was feeling very light-headed and he wasn't tracking well. Still, he was aware that there'd been a significant delay in the struggle, although he wasn't sure why. Maybe his enemies were fighting amongst themselves. That would be good.

He wasn't sure how long the delay had been. He thought he might have been, at best, semi-conscious for a good while after the last fight. If his enemies had had their act together, they could have killed him easily.

Malik heard the scrabbling that presaged another fighter climbing to the roof. He struggled to a sitting position and almost fainted from the pain of his crippled right arm. He used his left arm to lever himself up onto one knee. Through strength of will alone, he stood, his severed lifeline hanging behind him.

He hadn't been able to tie it back together with just one hand.

When the three warriors made their way to his side of the roof, they beheld Malik standing, swaying, yes, but still on his feet. His face was stained with soot and splattered with blood, which also darkened his entire right side and pooled around his feet. His hair was half burnt off. He looked like some maniacal demon silhouetted against the blue sky.

He threatened the three warriors with the eight inches of his broken sword in his left hand and roared, "Who wants to die first?"

His attackers spread out and deliberately started towards him. Then he saw them pause and look to their right with surprise. A second later, there was a painfully loud crack as lightning enveloped all three attackers and propelled them off the roof in a greasy cloud of disintegrating body parts.

Malik looked to his left and saw the King's secretary, Winton Marshfel, floating in midair.

An arrow flashed towards the diminutive secretary, but slowed and stopped an arm's length away. Winton looked at the south tower with an expression of annoyance. He gestured and a fireball materialized and sped toward the tower. There was an explosion outside Malik's view.

"What in the seven hells is going on here?" Winton demanded. Then he spotted the basket. "Is that the princess?"

Malik fell backward, unable to stand any longer.

"Yes," he said. "That's the princess."

"The Queen?"

"Dead. Everybody's dead, except maybe Melly, if they didn't cut her throat right away. They had inside help. Kashmal rebels, led by a local man named Razmar. You really, really want to talk to him if you can find him."

"Yes," said Winton, pursing his lips. "I think we have much to discuss."

He floated over the roof to the princess. Her basket lifted into the air to meet Winton. He waved diffidently and her basket's lifeline obediently untied itself. He grabbed her basket and turned back to face Malik.

"Lydio, you rest for a few minutes. I'll be back for you."

With that, Winton and the princess disappeared with a pop.

Melly saw Pandomar look up sharply at what sounded like thunder outside. He turned to Razmar and said, "I believe we have overstayed our welcome."

"What?" Razmar looked at him disdainfully. "What do you mean?"

"You've not been to war, have you?"

"What's that have to do with—"

Pandomar said softly, "You'd know the sounds you hear when the mages show up and all hope is lost."

Melly kept her face impassive, but inside, she exulted. The princess was safe! She could only hope that Malik was safe, too. She was much less sure of her own safety, however.

The tension in the room was thick, but she could sense a change in the dynamic between Pandomar and Razmar. In some indefinable way, she could feel the mantle of leadership settling around Pandomar.

Pandomar turned away from Razmar and walked over to the prone form of his son. He reached out and cupped his son's cheek tenderly with one hand.

Without looking at Razmar, Pandomar said, "Kill him."

"Wait, you can't—"

Two of his warriors stepped up to Razmar and immobilized his arms. While the traitor struggled ineffectively, a third fighter stepped up behind him and cut his throat with a broad knife. Blood spurted into the air, and the two warriors holding him let his body drop unceremoniously to the floor.

Pandomar walked over and stood in front of Melly. She was tied to the chair and could do nothing but look up at him defiantly.

"He knew too much to be left alive," he said. "And you...this was all a waiting game, wasn't it?"

"Yes," she answered, looking up at him and refusing to show her fear.

"Well played."

Pandomar bowed slightly, then he and his men exited the room and ran for their lives.

Miska lay on the floor, fortunately unconscious for the proceedings. The healer, a wizened grandmother in a maroon robe, had finally managed to get the arrow out of the red ruin of his eye socket.

Looking up at Danteel, Orlik, and the other six surviving volunteer fighters standing around them, she said, "He's lucky he turned when he did. The arrow ruined his nose bridge, and the eye's a total loss, but it smashed the eye socket apart and exited rather than going into his brain."

Danteel saw Orlik breathe a sigh of relief. His son was going to live.

"The biggest problem," the healer continued, "is going to be infection." She paused, looking around. "I'm not too worried about that, though. When it comes to healing, I'm just a minor Talent. When the King finds out what you've done, I'm sure he'll make his Royal Healer available. She's got the power to fix all of this."

"All right, I've got you, Lydio. Stay with me."

Malik was dimly aware of his surroundings. Strangely, he felt like he was floating, which was odd. He felt cold, and a shiver shook his frame, which hurt and reminded him that he was still maybe slightly alive even if his head was full of cobwebs.

Now he was moving through a crowd of Salasian soldiers and a few Phoenix Guardsmen who parted before him. For some reason, they were all saluting with their right fists clinched over their heart. He wondered who they were saluting. He was still wondering when he lost consciousness.

XVII. LATER

One doesn't have to play well, it's enough to play better than your opponent.

— Sigbart Forester, Chess Scholar, from Tarrasch

"Sire," Winton said. "I have the final tally for you."

King Salzari nodded, his visage devoid of emotion. Winton had known his liege lord for over thirty years and recognized his friend's pain, even if he was covering it up as much as possible. Soldiers, guardsmen, various functionaries, and advisors surrounded them.

Now that Winton's secret was out of the bag, the oh-so-carefully hidden secret that he was a powerful, unregistered combat mage, the secret that he and King Salzari had hidden for so many years, people were looking at him much differently. He'd gone from being a funny-looking fop to a significant threat in just a single day. Nobody was quite sure how to treat him anymore.

"There were one-hundred and fifty-four raiders," Winton said. "Two of them were captured by local volunteers."

"We will want to meet the volunteers and see that they are rewarded for their service."

"Indeed, sire, they also played a critical role in saving the princess."

Salzari raised an eyebrow, then nodded.

"Fourteen were captured during the final pursuit, after I brought a cohort through." A cohort was about five hundred men, a tenth of a legion. Bad enough that he'd had to reveal that he was a mage. Opening and sustaining a portal revealed to anybody with any knowledge of magic that he was at least a Beta, the second highest ranking of a mage's power. "The rest are dead, except for their leader, a warrior named Pandomar, who appears to have escaped."

Salzari went still, which those close to him knew was never a good sign. "How?"

"He was apparently a shifter." Winton paused. "I'm sorry, sire." Salzari waved his hand, his signal for moving on. "He presents as a black and tan mountain panther with three legs. There were sightings, but we didn't put it together until it was too late. He escaped through the city and disappeared into the wilderness."

Looking around, Salzari said, "We want him dead. Put a price on his head that will make him the most wanted man in the Thousand Kingdoms."

"They were accompanied by a combat mage," Winton said. "A Gamma, based on my evaluation of his performance. He was killed during the takeover of Paksenaral."

Salzari nodded.

The King had already been briefed on Chently's heroic actions, but there was no need to make Chently's name, or the fact that he'd been a mage, known to the court. There were already people wondering how many other hidden mages Salzari had.

In actuality, Chently had gotten lucky and taken out a more powerful, but less fresh, mage by surprise, though he hadn't survived.

Looking around, Winton continued. "I think it's common knowledge by now that the Kashmal attackers had inside help, orchestrated by Tulis Razmar. We have truth scryers checking to see if anybody else was involved, though that's not my area of responsibility. I'm just a secretary."

There were a few titters from the audience, quickly subdued.

Salzari stood up. Addressing the crowd, he said, "We will return home to arrange the Queen's funeral. When we return, we will settle the Kashmal problem."

He turned and strode from the room.

Sometime later, Malik awakened in a soft, comfortable bed. He didn't feel any pain anymore. He tried moving his arms and legs in turn and was pleased to see that they all seemed to respond.

"Malik?"

He heard Melly's voice and turned towards her. She was sitting in a chair next to the bed.

"The princess?" he croaked.

"She's fine," Melly said.

His princess was fine.

His.

He nodded and fell asleep again.

Did You Like This Book?

Please let everyone know by posting a review on any of your favorite online retailers. Reviews are vital for authors in today's media-driven world.

Do You Want More?

Sign up for my monthly newsletter for news about future releases, plus get one of my near-future SF novelettes, *The Jakarta Breach*, for free when you sign up.

`www.davidkeener.org/newsletter`

And don't forget...

I've got a bunch of **Extras** for
you on the following pages.

EXTRAS

Afterward

Find out more about how *The Rooftop Game* came to be created and the inspirations behind the story.

Thousand Kingdoms Timeline

A Timeline of all the currently published, or soon-to-be-published, stories set within the loosely connected *Thousand Kingdoms* series.

BONUS STORY: Winter Roses

"Winter Roses" is the first short story set in the Thousand Kingdoms that was ever published, way back in 2015.

PREVIEW: Bitter Days

Check out Chapter 1 of *Bitter Days*, David Keener's next thrilling publication in the series.

AFTERWARD

About the Setting

The Thousand Kingdoms was my idea for a sprawling fantasy canvas, a vast common setting where I could tell a bunch of different stories...and different *types* of stories. I didn't flesh it out all at once, of course, but I did establish some broad guidelines for the setting.

It's what they call a second-world fantasy setting, meaning that it's a fantasy world that's not a variant of Earth or some specific period in Earth's history.

In the Thousand Kingdoms, first-rank mages, the Alphas, are extremely powerful and dangerous, and thus rule everything, but there aren't very many of them. So they keep society organized into lots of separate little kingdoms and even encourage a bit of anarchy...as long as trade doesn't get interrupted.

My goal was to be able to write a bunch of stories without having to do too much in the way of time-consuming world-building for each new story.

Of course, I failed miserably at that.

What really happened is that I *still* do world-building for *every* story in the setting. It's just that each new story contributes new details to the overall canvas, hopefully making it deeper and richer while still maintaining internal consistency. Essentially, I'm building a detailed setting by accretion, story by story, bounded by my original guidelines.

About the Characters

People generally read stories because of interesting characters, not settings. Don't believe me? How many of you have read *The Lord of the Rings*? Now, how many of you have read Tolkien's *The Silmarillion*?

Right. I rest my case.

I had a setting. Now I needed characters.

My next inspiration, to some degree, was the Marvel comic books I'd read when I was growing up. It also didn't hurt that the Marvel Cinematic Universe (MCU) was pretty much tearing up the box office at the movie theaters when I started writing seriously (however, the Thousand Kingdoms setting actually sprang out of the GURPS Fantasy gaming my friends and I engaged in starting in the mid '90s).

As with Marvel's comic books, I thought it would be fun if I could arrange to have some of my characters cross into each other's stories. I also envisioned a variety of unique heroes…and villains.

Lots of characters, like…the Royal Bodyguard (who evolved into the paranoid and stubborn Lydio Malik). And Tavish Kraigdu, the retired Legionnaire and sometime blacksmith who seems to get pulled into solving crimes (he's the main character of an upcoming story called "Death Comes to Town"). And Chaga, the Faceless Assassin. Winton Marshfel, the hidden combat mage (star of a future story tentatively called "Unleashed"). Pageeda, a homeless street child in a gritty port city, who must solve a horrifying crime (see "Bitter Days").

And more.

About The Story

The first published story in my Thousand Kingdoms setting was "Winter Roses" in 2015, a very short story included as an extra in this volume. The second was "The Rooftop Game," originally published in an anthology in 2017.

For *The Rooftop Game*, I wanted to take Lydio Malik, whom I'd envisioned as a highly competent and ruthless bodyguard…and make him a complete and total underdog. Not just against the bad guys, but even with his own side.

I had two major influences.

The classic action movie, *Die Hard*, is a fairly obvious one, I think, at least to me. When I first described the story to my writing group, I even pitched it as "*Die Hard*...on the roof of a castle tower."

The second was Jackie Robinson, the first African-American baseball player in professional baseball.

I made Lydio Malik a foreigner from Neferia, a land of dark-skinned people (think of him as a dark-skinned Indian). I also made him the first Neferian to become a Phoenix Guard member. He is ridiculed by his compatriots for his heritage and his unorthodox views on how bodyguards should carry out their duties.

In a way, the story is about Malik proving to himself, and everybody else, that he has what it takes to be the Royal Bodyguard for Princess Analisa.

About Chess

I knew that I wanted this story to have a strong chess theme running through it. However, as stylized as it might be, chess is a war game. As such, it had to be at least somewhat different in the Thousand Kingdoms. There's no way a war game could ignore the power of the mages that ruled society.

Hence, the Mage piece, seen to the side, which replaces one of the Bishops. Based on the variant Capablanca chess rules, the Mage piece combines the Bishop's diagonal movement with the Knight's more tactical movement.

Try it. You might just find yourself enjoying chess in the Thousand Kingdoms style.

I had a lot of fun writing "The Rooftop Game." I sincerely hope you were entertained by it, too (you're not one of those people that skips to the end and reads all the extras first, are you?).

Rest assured, I've got more plans for Lydio Malik. And Melly, Pandomar, Princess Analisa, and Winton Marshfel, as well.

David Keener
March 21, 2018
Ashburn, Virginia

THOUSAND KINGDOMS TIMELINE

A number of my existing stories, and a bunch of upcoming ones, all exist in a setting that I call the Thousand Kingdoms. In many cases, the primary characters from one story may appear in other stories. Within that setting, here's a Timeline for the stories that have either been published or are completed and soon to appear.

Year	Story	Sub-Series
1318	*Bitter Days*	Pageeda & Scuffee
1318	*Death Goes to a Ball*	Faceless Assassin
1318	*Death Comes to Town*	Faceless Assassin
1317	*Jonelle Crosse*	Jonelle Crosse
1316	*Last Day on the Job*	Royal Defenders
1308	*The Rooftop Game*	Royal Defenders
1280	*Chess Lessons*	
1271	*Stone Spirits*	Paladins of Orellanna
1216	*Winter Roses*	

Lydio Malik, the royal bodyguard from this book, also appears in the story "Last Day on the Job."

Stories within any of the sub-series should be read in chronological order; otherwise, any reading order works.

WINTER ROSES

My darling, are you awake?

I see that you are. I can see your eyes tracking me as I move.

Can you understand me? Try to blink once for 'Yes,' and twice for 'No.'

Well done. I thought I might be too late, my darling ...I'm sorry; that was insensitive. My words are clumsy, my manners uncultured by your standard. I have little call for courtly manners and flowery language here in my mountain kingdom.

There were...things...that I had to attend to, or I'd never have left your side. I am so sorry about your affliction. I never expected this. I wish, for your sake, that I'd never brought you back to my harsh realm. It hurts me so much to see you like this, so pale and still.

I remember when I first saw you. I'd come down from the mountains to resolve some landholder and right-of-passage disputes with Count Scolatari. He'd insisted on hosting one of his balls while I was there, to distract me from the negotiations, I thought at the time.

I'd not have attended, but my advisors had been hounding me, claiming that at twenty-five I was too long without a wife and an heir to secure the Cragenrath lineage. "Seek out suitable candidates," I was advised.

I was introduced to dozens of hopeful young women at that extravagant celebration. Then I saw you across the hall, holding a crowd of onlookers entranced with your sparkling wit, shaking your raven tresses with merriment. I was lost to anyone else before ever we spoke.

And when I did introduce myself, you made me feel sophisticated, even though I knew I was not. I was thrilled to discover that you had a keen intelligence, and that you had read most of the books I had read, and many that I had not. Books have always helped my family get through our howling winters.

I was even more surprised when I learned of your modest skills with the sword. I eagerly volunteered to instruct you further in your swordsmanship, a skill that you took to readily, and far more gracefully than I.

I stayed long at Scolatari's keep, and when I left, I asked you to accompany me. I asked you to share my mountain realm with me, to be my wife. I was overjoyed when you said "Yes." It was the happiest I have ever been.

I wish now that I had never succumbed to your charms, because it brought you to this.

I'd rather have had a wistful memory of a long-ago dalliance than this cruel reality that lies before us now.

When you arrived, I introduced you to my family and retainers. I gifted you with the ring you now wear, a family heirloom of immense value. Everyone was impressed with your beauty, your polished ways, your wit. Everyone was overjoyed to meet you.

Nobody was more surprised than I when you fell ill the very next day. Surely, it must be just a simple sickness, easily abolished. But as you grew weaker, it became clear that you had fallen to the Curse of Cragenrath.

I am young, I know. But I am not stupid. The Curse only falls upon those who seek to harm Cragenrath. I never expected this and, obviously, neither did you.

I investigated further. It didn't take me long to discover your compatriots.

AND YOUR HUSBAND!

I'm sorry. In the state you're in, it's unfair of me to shout at you.

Yes, I found your fellow plotters: the scholarly ex-monk and your husband, a mercenary from Brylandia. I quickly identified the monk as the weaker of the two, and we broke him within a few hours.

I was appalled when I learned how you studied me. Discovered my likes and my weaknesses.

Guessed at my innermost desires. Your husband, using his roguish charm to extract information from strangers. The ex-monk, with his talent for research.

And you, with your acting skills. An accomplished stage actress from a far-off realm.

Everything you told me was a lie. Even your love was just an act.

The scholar didn't survive the interrogation. We threw his remains, unshriven, off a cliff. May his ghost haunt the mountains in torment.

And your husband…oh, how I hated him. He had your love, and I did not. But I had no choice in the matter. Honor stands above us all.

For the sake of what could have been, I gave him a fighting chance. We fought a duel. That I am here must tell you that he lost.

I can attest, though, that he fought bravely, and was more of a challenge than I had expected. He even gave me a minor scratch. But I am a warrior from the line of warriors that tamed these mountains. I have been trained from childhood by some of the finest swordsmen who ever lived.

He fell with my sword in his stomach. I could have let him suffer in agony for so long as it should take him to die. However, we lords of the mountains are ruthless, but not overly cruel. I gave him mercy and, for your sake, even buried him in the manner of his people.

The ironic thing is that you and your companions were seeking to steal the treasure of Cragenrath. My darling, you're wearing it right now, the ring I gave you when you arrived.

My ancestor seventeen generations agone was a wizard. He crafted a magical heirloom, an ornate, jeweled ring. Our tradition is to gift it to anyone who seeks to join our clan. Those who intend us harm die an agonizing and withering death that we call the Curse of Cragenrath. Sadly, the Curse is inexorable once it begins, and the ring can't be removed without the magical backblast incinerating everything in this room.

My ancestor wrought far too well.

I've picked out a spot for you, overlooking the view you found so stunning when you first arrived. I'll plant our famous winter roses above your grave. They have great white flowers and leaves so dark they're almost black. Hidden beneath the leaves are the thorns. Treachery hiding underneath beauty.

Strangely fitting, I think.

I'm sorry that it has come to this. I still love you, you know.

Even now, I'd set you free if I could. I wish things could have been different.

Rest now, my darling. The pain will be gone soon.

Author's Afterward

"Winter Roses" is the first short story set in the Thousand Kingdoms milieu that I ever completed, and takes place several generations before *The Rooftop Game*. It's an admittedly odd story, originally done as an almost Shakespearean ten-minute speech for Toastmasters, an international club dedicated to helping members improve their public speaking (including old-fashioned storytelling).

In a very real way, this story, and the positive reaction to my storytelling, was responsible for re-igniting my Dream of being a professional writer. It was originally written in 2012 and later professionally published in anthologies in 2015 and 2017.

PREVIEW

Turn the page for an excerpt from *Bitter Days*, the next exciting story in the Thousand Kingdoms series from David Keener.

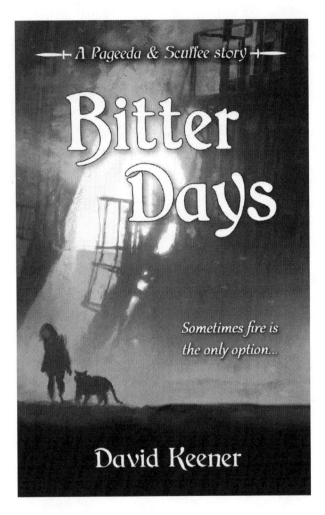

A Pageeda & Scuffee story

Bitter Days

Sometimes fire is the only option...

David Keener

A homeless girl living in a gritty port city struggles to hunt down the men who kidnapped her older sister. She's assisted by a young but strangely intelligent and oversized cat.

I. A Festival to Remember

Of regrets, I have only this, that I shall never again experience Cosaturi's Festival of Lights for the first time, for I have seen the heavens kiss the Urth and am forever changed.

— Bakil Tesar, from *Around the Thousand Kingdoms, Vol. XIII*

"I want to see it all!" shouted Pageeda, dragging her older sister by the hand through the throng of festivalgoers. Pageeda used her smaller size to wiggle through the crowd. Illyria, three years older and a head taller than Pageeda, had a tougher time and found herself repeatedly apologizing as she bumped into people. Finally, Pageeda managed to secure them a position at the front of the jostling crowd so they could see the parade as it passed.

The waterfront was the last leg of the Parade of Lights, which had already wound its way through the richer areas of the city where street people like Pageeda and Illyria were not welcome. To Illyria's cynical eyes, the performers looked tired and a little bored. But one look at Pageeda's shiny face told Illyria that all her sister saw was the magic, just as she'd hoped. Pageeda looked up at her, smiling and laughing.

Pageeda clapped her hands with delight as a team of barrel walkers rolled by. Each performer danced and jumped on top of a five-foot-tall rolling barrel, playing to the crowd. A team of three muscular men pulled each barrel along using a loop of rope running through a circular track in the barrel. Pageeda looked up at her and said, "The barrel's like a giant pulley that they're pulling along. That's so clever."

Illyria didn't have the heart to tell her that all the barrel dancers were probably slaves. Pageeda would find out soon enough that everything in this city had its dark side.

The barrel dancers were followed by a crew of tumbling acrobats, a wagon carrying a band of musicians playing a popular jig, and more, all greeted with enthusiasm by Pageeda, hopping up and down with such excitement that the people around them were smiling and laughing at her. One man even gave Pageeda some delicious leftover pastries, dripping with some sort of sweet frosting, which she shared with Illyria. Typically, street people were all but invisible to the denizens of the Zanya, but everything was different during the festival.

During festival week, people were happy, often drunk, and surprisingly free with coins. Illyria and

Pageeda had collected quite a few coins this past week, despite not having been able to get near any of the highly coveted begging spots. Even better, food was plentiful, and leftovers were easy to find. Sometimes people even gave away food, like the man who'd given Pageeda the pastries, which was much better than pulling scraps out of the garbage like usual. Festival meant full bellies for them, the opportunity to taste foods they'd normally never get to sample, and life was a little easier for a short time.

They watched one spectacle after another as the parade wended past, until all of the acts blurred together in a sort of sensory overload. There were Salasian soldiers marching in unison; a strident marching band; an ornately decorated wagon with a bevy of beauties posing provocatively to advertise a prominent brothel; a troop of mounted, black-skinned horsemen from the Zenophan plains; more acrobats, this time from far-off Rusitania, doing a twirling dance; and a ponderous, doublewide wagon trimmed in blue bunting and pulled by twelve white horses that represented the Church of Turkos. A black-robed wizard with long black hair and a neatly trimmed beard stood near the front of the wagon, just above a large brass figure of a serpent arranged in a figure-eight to look like it was eating its own tail. Waving his arms theatrically, he conjured brilliantly colored apparitions of fantastic beasts and mythical creatures that cavorted in the air with wild abandon until they popped like soap bubbles high in the air. Turkosian temple soldiers in chain mail marched beside the wagon, all of them white-skinned with black hair.

While many in the crowd cheered loudly when the wagon came into view, many did not. Neferian refugees, who'd lost their homeland to forces aided by Turkosian mercenaries, were common in this quarter, and many looked on with bitter, angry, or defiant expressions. Some of the more daring souls even turned their backs to the wagon as it passed by.

The Turkosians were a relatively recent addition to Zanya, having begun appearing in the city about a decade ago, around the time that Illyria and her pregnant mother had arrived as refugees from the Neferian civil war. After building their influence for several years, the Turkosians acquired the rights to Temple Hill, one of the three hills around which South Cosaturi was built, and promptly leveled the entire area to build their fortress-like temple compound. Thousands of people had been ruthlessly displaced, many of them Neferian refugees.

Illyria, Pageeda, and their mother had been among the displaced, which may also have been a contributing factor to the sickness that took their mother from them shortly thereafter. Illyria couldn't help but think that the ever-increasing power of the Turkosians didn't bode well for Cosaturi.

Pageeda felt Illyria tugging on her hand. She pulled herself away from the spectacle of the parade to look at her sister and saw that she was pointing at some of their friends, street kids like themselves, who were waving at them from a nearby rooftop on their side of the street. Pageeda reluctantly let Illyria pull her back through the crowd.

As they neared the edge of the crowd, Pageeda heard a man shouting, "Never forget!" in a loud voice. She tugged free of Illyria's hand and darted through the throng, grinning as Illyria struggled not to lose sight of her in the crowd.

The voice belonged to an older man with hair that might once have been black but was now mostly gray, and a scraggly beard that reached down to his chest. "Never forget!" he shouted in a loud, quavering voice. "I fought for you!" He was sitting on the ground, right leg stretched out in front of him, and the other just a stump that ended at the knee. His right hand was also missing, and there was a nasty scar that cut across the left side of his face.

A passerby dropped a few coins in a small, wicker bowl before him, then walked on. The man said in a lower tone of voice, "Thank you, sir. You are a patriot."

Pageeda stopped in front of the man. With her hands on her hips, she asked, "Never forget what?"

A hand came to rest on her shoulder as Illyria stepped up behind her.

The old man glanced briefly at Illyria and then brought his gaze back to Pageeda. "Never forget those who fought for this city and this nation. I fought at the Battle of Antigon. That's where I lost these." He gestured with his left hand, encompassing his missing right hand and the stump of his left leg. "For what I've given up for these people, they can spare a few coins now and then."

Pageeda pulled a small coin from her pocket and dropped it in the man's basket. The man laughed roughly, then reached into the basket and handed the coin back to her. "Girl, you need that coin more than I do. I'll take money from them's that can afford it. But I thank you, nevertheless."

Pageeda let Illyria pull her away from the beggar. As the man receded behind them, they heard him exhorting the crowd once more: "Never forget!"

Illyria clutched Pageeda's hand as they walked into a narrow alley that smelled like refuse. Pageeda wrinkled her nose as they stepped from bright sunlight into the dimness. Pageeda stopped abruptly, yanking Illyria to a halt.

Some sort of odd-looking cat was lying partially on top of a foot-long rat that it had clearly just killed. It snarled at them, showing a mouthful of white fangs that looked larger and sharper than those of a normal feline. As Pageeda's eyes adjusted, she noticed that its fur was dirty, clumped with what looked like tar or something sticky. It was some sort of cat, but like nothing Pageeda had ever seen. It was more than twice the size of a large alley cat, or about half Pageeda's size, and had outsized ears, large eyes, and huge paws.

Illyria was on Pageeda's right side, closer to the beast. Pageeda pulled Illyria away from the dangerous-looking predator. Pageeda looked straight into the eyes of the cat and said, "Nice kitty. We don't want your rat. You have nothing to worry about."

Pageeda nudged her sister in an arc that skirted around the strange beast and its fresh kill. Pageeda never took her eyes off its face as they navigated around it, and the animal craned its neck so that it never took its eyes off her as they passed by.

A short distance further down the alley, they climbed up on some wooden boxes that were leaning up against a building, clambered up to the first-floor roof, and then shimmied up a wooden drainpipe that creaked in protest to reach the next level. Moments later, hand-in-hand, they joined their friends, Melis, Jamsin, and Felichuk, on their perch overlooking the street.

Melis greeted them with a cheery "Hello," and a wave. She was Illyria's best friend, a pretty, dark-haired girl a year older than Illyria. Whenever she had extra food, which wasn't often these days, she'd share it with Illyria, always saying that it was for Pageeda.

Pageeda rushed forward and hugged Melis. "Hi, Melis," she said. "Hi, Jamsin." With his long blond hair and fair skin, thirteen-year-old Jamsin was the only one of their group who wasn't of Neferian descent. She pointedly left out a greeting for Felichuk, who was sitting beyond Jamsin.

Sitting beside Melis, Jamsin grinned and waved distractedly, occupied with another of his little wooden animal carvings. He'd acquired a small, six-inch knife a couple of years ago, although he wouldn't say how. To pass the time, he'd started carving driftwood into animal shapes like the carvings he'd always admired in the marketplace; by now, he was actually fairly decent. He'd even given a couple of his little carvings to Pageeda.

"What are you working on, Jamsin?" Pageeda asked.

Jamsin smiled at her and held up his latest carving, a four-inch-long dolphin, generally held as a symbol of good luck by the folk of Cosaturi. Since he wasn't done carving it yet, the poor dolphin looked like it was desperately trying to leap out of a piece of gray, weathered driftwood.

"I sold one of 'em yesterday for four coppers. I think the man what bought it thought he was getting something I stole from a shop."

Pageeda and Illyria laughed appreciatively; the others had already heard the story.

Felichuk said, "Hey, Illyria, how's it going?" He was a short, scrappy boy who had begun to annoy Pageeda with his constant efforts to impress her sister. He was always bragging about being an up-and-coming trainee for Pomaya's gang of thieves. Pageeda didn't think that being a trainee was worth bragging about, plus it seemed like kind of a bad idea to advertise about being a thief.

"It's been a good day," Illyria replied. "It's Pageeda's tenth birthday, so I've been taking her all around."

"My birthday's two days after Princess Analisa's," Pageeda interjected. "Only she's two years older than me."

"Big deal," said Felichuk. "It's not like you're ever going to meet her." Melis reached around Jamsin's back and swatted Felichuk in the head, eliciting a giggle from Pageeda, who was otherwise pretending that Felichuk didn't exist.

"I like your ribbon, Illyria," Melis said, casting an envious glance at Illyria's neck.

Illyria grinned. Pageeda knew she'd been looking forward to showing it off ever since she'd found the bright red ribbon on the ground a few days before, still in good shape despite being trampled by who knew how many people. Selma the Seamstress had sewed it on her tan-colored shift for free. The ribbon encircled the neck opening of her outfit; the ends were tied in a bow in front. For street kids, it was the height of fashion.

The five of them watched the parade for a while, Pageeda leaning comfortably back on the sloped roof while Illyria and Melis conversed beside her. At dusk, lights appeared throughout the city, all the normal lights of a city at night, plus thousands of lights put up in honor of the Festival of Lights.

"This is my favorite part of the festival, the nighttime lights," Illyria said. "It's like the city we know has been replaced by some magical city where anything is possible."

"Same dirty city." Melis shrugged. "Just better lit."

Pageeda pointed as she spotted the first rocket climbing skyward from its launch point on the Crescent, the rocky arc of land that sheltered Zanya's harbor from ocean storms. Before Illyria could respond to Melis, the first of the evening fireworks detonated in an elaborate starburst high in the sky above the Bay of Fools. They watched the fireworks show in companionable silence until it ended in a rousing climax of thunderous, multi-colored explosions.

"I meant to tell you earlier, we saw this really strange cat in the alley right before we climbed up here," Illyria said. "It looked really vicious."

Melis said, "Cream-colored, kind of dirty, with big ears?"

"Yes."

"I've seen it around lately," Melis said. "Didn't look too dangerous to me."

"You didn't see its teeth."

Pageeda looked at them. "He wasn't dangerous," she said. "He was just really hungry, and he didn't want us to steal his dinner. And he was sad because he was all alone."

Melis said, "Pageeda, you can't know that."

"I can, too," she insisted.

Melis just smiled and shook her head, letting the matter drop.

Illyria changed the subject to general gossip about the people they knew. After a while, they said their goodbyes, and then climbed back down to the alley. As Illyria led them home, a light rain began to fall. Pageeda was so tired that she could barely stumble along holding Illyria's hand. Within a short time, they arrived at the alley where they'd been staying for the last few weeks. Home was a hidden shelter behind a modestly upscale cafe called the Hestrian Grotto.

Pageeda didn't realize anything was wrong until it was too late. Between the soft patter of rainfall that muffled any other noises and her tiredness she was caught unaware as three men wearing dark, hooded cloaks stepped out of the shadows and blocked their path. Pageeda pulled Illyria backward, but stopped as two more ambushers appeared behind them.

Pageeda froze, paralyzed with fear. While she hesitated, Illyria charged at the man directly in front of them. At the last second, she darted left. The center man tried to grab her but couldn't get a hold of her rain-slick body. She screamed and leaped on the left-most man, viciously scratching his eyes and face with her fingernails until he toppled backward.

Illyria looked up. Pageeda had followed her, and was trying to help. She grabbed Pageeda's arm and yanked her through the gap she'd created in the ring of attackers. "Run, Pageeda! Run!"

Pageeda stumbled and fell hard enough to stun her for a moment. She saw Illyria attack another man, but someone else grabbed her sister in a chokehold from behind and lifted her off the ground. Still screaming, Illyria kicked the man in front of her and savagely bit the arm of her choker.

Pageeda bounced to her feet and started to run, but another ambusher loomed above her and grabbed her arm. He was thin and wiry, with a grip like a steel band. She noticed that a few strands of long, dark hair had escaped from beneath his hood.

She pulled her only weapon from her pocket, a piece of sharp glass from a broken bottle, and slashed her attacker's arm. As he yelled in pain, she tried to pull away, but his grip was too strong. She slashed at his face only to have him bat her hand away, sending the glass shard flying. He yanked her towards him and tried to immobilize her in a bear hug.

She head-butted him as hard as she could and heard a satisfying crunch. Half-dazed, she clawed her way out of his loosened grip. Her hand got caught in the folds of his tunic; there was a ripping sound, and she was free.

She ran for her life.

She heard Illyria screaming behind her as she ran until, with awful suddenness, the screaming stopped.

ABOUT THE AUTHOR

Aboard a mock-up of the Space Shuttle Atlantis.

David Keener is an author, editor, and public speaker who lives in Northern Virginia with his wife and two, oops, three, inordinately large dogs. He writes SF, Fantasy, and Mystery but loves the idea of mashing up his favorite genres in new and unexpected ways.

He is the grand instigator behind the *Worlds Enough* anthology series, and co-editor of the first two volumes, *Fantastic Defenders* and *Fantastic Detectives*. His next anthology will be *The Forever Inn*, about a mysterious inn that travels randomly throughout the multiverse.

He is a founding member of the *Hourlings Podcast Project,* covering writing-related topics. He frequently speaks at conventions, where he often conducts writing workshops. Find out more about him at:

Newsletter: www.davidkeener.org/newsletter
Website: www.davidkeener.org
Facebook: DavidKeenerWrites

ACKNOWLEDGMENTS

A surprisingly large number of people helped me with *The Rooftop Game*, including: Bill Aguiar, Chris Anderson, Don Anderson, John Dwight, Mary Ellen Gavin, Stephanie Groot, Elizabeth Hayes, Jeremy Holloway, Jeffrey C. Jacobs, Sally Keener, Bill Krieger, Amanda Kryway, Lou Lamoureux, Joanne McAlpine, Shea Megale, Asher Roth, Donna Royston, Brigitta Rubin, and Martin Wilsey.

A futuristic heist behind enemy lines, featuring a team of art historians and mercenaries. What could possibly go wrong?

A story in the *Inflection Point* universe.

CREDITS

Front Cover Art: From SelfPubBookCovers.com, used under license.

Chess Piece Images: From Microvector, licensed from Creative Market (creativemarket.com); modifications by David Keener.

Paw Print: Licensed from Deposit Photos; modifications by David Keener.

Sword Separator Icon (Full & Broken): From Vector Shop, licensed from Creative Market (creativemarket.com); modifications by David Keener.

Tower Photo: CC0, from maxpixel.greatpicture.com; modifications by David Keener.

Made in the USA
Columbia, SC
13 October 2024

43663796R00086